KILL THE PUNKS

KILL THE PUNKS

A Hated Youth Memoir

John Oliver Hodges

Wasp Leg Press

ISBN: 979-8-9938775-0-1

For Eric Rodgers 1964–2025

Note: this is Part One of a trilogy crafted through memory. As memory is fallible, subject to fable, so is it true of this narrative. Though the recollections of those interviewed, as well as the official record as documented in newspaper and magazine articles, flyers from shows, albums and photographs, have been closely consulted, the fictive nature of memory remains. Some names of people and places have been changed. That alone would indicate that this is fiction.

WARNING: this book contains transgressive themes, and includes depictions of drug use, bullying, homophobia, racism, sexism, brutal fantasies, sexual violence, and crime. Please use discretion.

JOHN OLIVER HODGES was born in Florida, and was the guitarist for Hated Youth in 1981, when the band formed, until 1984, when the band disbanded. His published works of fiction include *The Love Box* (Livingston Press); *Luv Slaps* (Broken Tribe Press); and *Bulgasari Nightmare* (Anxiety Press) written under the pen-name Opham Denyer.

CONTENTS

Search my soul, but nothing's there, nothing but air. How in the hell do you find yourself, when there's no one there?

—Eric Rodgers

Preface

Howdy.

How I will start this is:

We were Big Mama Hardcore's suckling mess of malnourished sickly runts, not so brawn compared to bands coming out of Boston and New York. In Austin and Detroit photos were taken at the shows. People filmed. And in Chicago and Long Beach records were bonded, flown overseas. Hardcore punk personalities emerged as regional specimens of the genre, bold dogs like Metal Mike and Mike Muir and Fat Mike before he was called Fat Mike. There was Mike Ness, Roger Miret, and Jello Biafra. Can anybody say Mike Sversvold? How about Vic Bondi or John Brannon? These brutes in punk had shit to shout.

We too had shit to shout. Even had a leader of the pack, Hated Eric whose voice was loud, go figure. He lifted weights and owned a moniker. He screwed the girls and hoarded the spotlight on every occasion. I would put Hated

Eric up there with all of the "great punks." I would like to put those punks in a chain-link cage with Eric, one at a time, even Henry Rollins, even that scary-looking muscle guy from the Misfits. In these fight-to-the-death battles I'd bet on Eric, guaranteed to be the last man standing, the ultimate punk smattered with blood from ripping those other guys limb from limb. He was bold and bad and bald and ready to brain you with a brick.

Though Hated Eric was interviewed, nothing you might call a philosophy spouted out of wee us. Why would it have? We were 15 and 16. What did we know? In truth we could only pretend to know. Unlike the Bad Brains who seemed to know what they were screaming about, promoting their Positive Mental Attitude shtick that they picked up somewhere or other, we had no official message. Minor Threat had their Let's Be Squares, aka *Straight Edge* business on the make while the Meatmen were getting down and dirty in the psychosexual side of things: "We love it when girls shit on our faces." JFA said *Let's skate and eat junk food and take big bong hits by the sea*, a modern-day Beach Boys, they were, with a thrash sound. These bands were wonderful great fun. They drummed out notions of how things were and how things should be and put on great shows.

Sift through lyrics of any eighties' hardcore album and you'll find themes suggesting a coherent point of view, a distinct flavor, but the punks have grown up, have had kids, have gone into jobs painting, welding, teaching, cooking. Some went for PhDs or joined the military. Others got into tech, or became lawyers. We have our criminals, our addicts, our yoga instructors. A few of us committed suicide but mostly we blended into the woodwork. We became responsible citizens and contributors to society.

Not that that's good.

Incredibly, many of the old bands still tour the country, put out amazing new records and even make a living screaming and blasting and pounding and looking rad: D.R.I., 7 Seconds, Bad Religion, and the Descendents who sang/sing, "I don't wanna grow up," and maybe never did grow up, cahoots to them for practicing what they preach/preached. As old man Socrates reportedly said: *An honest man remains a child.*

Though Hated Youth had no shtick, we had a logo. I made it in 1981, a stick figure splashed onto white paper with black acrylic, nothing precious, this basic symbol of humankind like what you might see in a prehistoric cave. It said we existed and were ruthless yet clueless, in the developmental stage. We knew not where we were going nor why we were here, and nor did we care, so who knew but that we might bloody people up at our schools like we sang about in our songs or join the United States Army and kill people overseas. Maybe we'd go crazy, get put into the nearby Chattahoochee Mental Ward, or become cannibals, or politicians with a mind to blow shit up. No way to say for sure, but this we sang: "We're not Nazis, we're not terrorists, we're just people and we don't want the rest." The story in the song puts us at a show in Gainesville with machineguns. We slide open the door of Eric's van and start mowing down the punks and our fans with big fat bullets—*daht daht daht daht daht*—bloodying them up nice and good. These were the folks who'd come to see us play. *Kill kill kill!*

We just did not want to be like anybody—nobody in the world! We wanted to be people with nothing in common with each other, some kind of aliens from outer space, which was impossible, right? We rejected mass media, people who hated Ronald Reagan, our parents and people who believed in forming communities. *Yuck!* We rejected the capitalist system along with every other system. Everything was for the reject pile, including ourselves. Education, brotherly love, none of it was trustworthy. To the Devil with it. Eviscerate Mr. Granola Cruncher! Hang Miss Touchy Feely from the rafters by her feet! Naked!

Our songs sprouted out of instinct readymade, almost without thought. We did not want to be good musicians. Never tried to become better at anything. To write a *good* song was never a goal. We merely did what we did, and despite our dumping of the world around us, we remained filters of it, a bowels of the culture, we vessels of emotion—STOP! I am taking liberties by saying "we." In truth I speak only for myself. My natural state was to have little to no self-awareness and maybe, just maybe all this business of rejecting everything in sight was me expressing my own feelings of having been rejected. I was born by mistake, did not fit in. I could feel. I sort of had a brain, but in ways it was like I did not exist.

I was very stupid. No joke.

I knew only that between ignorance and education I'd take ignorance. Between success and failure I'd take failure. Why? Because knowledge and adoration were qualities people I couldn't stand wanted bad and I did not want to be like them. I did not want to concede that my worth relied on anything other than *what* I was—an animal.

Though Hated Youth bit the tit of the national hard-core punk beast hard enough to pierce her vinyl aureole, causing her to trickle blood, Tallahassee evaded mention in the supposedly exhaustive documentary to come out in 2006, the one tracing hardcore's roots through interviews with folks like Dave Dictor of MDC, Harley Flanagan of Cro-Mags, Jack Grisham of T.S.O.L. and Keith Morris of the Circle Jerks. Whatever went down in Tallahassee was left out of the movie, and I would assume this kind of omission was true of numerous smalltime hardcore scenes all over the country, from tiny little towns to bigger cities that may have had a few odd attractions but no real universities. It wasn't until the internet was invented and started bringing people together in crisscross patterns from around the globe that Hated Youth and other underknown bands and scenes became accessible and admired by generations new and old.

What follows is the story of some guys you never heard of, myself one, who formed a band and played some shows and recorded some songs. When high school ended, and the band stopped playing, that's where the greater interest begins, because in the end, who cares about the music? "We care!" we all will shout in unison, "it was so meaningful to us, the times we had, the mischief, the girls, the guys we encountered during the magical eighties, even the food we ate," but music new and old in every genre hits us from all angles every day of the week, there's a constant flow of it. If you don't like one thing, you're going to latch on to something else. Ask me, more interesting than the music are the people who listen to it, who support it, who make it and the paths through life they take over it.

When it was over, the runt litter that was Hated Youth separated. We all wobbled off different ways. But we could not extricate ourselves from ourselves. The days when we'd worked together as a single entity, all cuddly in the soft embrace of Mama Hardcore, had shaped us. Though we may have been distant physically, our punk drama continued. Psychologically we were stuck with each other. *Stuck!*

A problem with punk memoirs and biographies of bands in general runs thus: there's the us we were and the us we remember. The us we were was a whole lot stupider, a whole lot more elemental, rawer than the us we've become, so we rewrite memories to give our earlier selves traits we didn't have. Pick up a punk memoir or documentary of a music scene and you'll find our old selves described as alienated souls seeking a tribe to thrive in, or as young renegades, people who see through lies or as conscientious youth aware of the evils of capitalism, conformity, communism, whatever. Even in grittier, seemingly more honest testimonies, we sense infection stemming from a will to the heroic. Because our brains were fresh out of childhood, we were either repeating canned ideas passed onto us from somewhere—hip parents, trends in music, historical tidbits—or performing the loathsome and embarrassing task of creating an identity. Who am I? NO THANK YOU!

In response to the above "problem" I retain the jejune and foolish, and provide signals of maturity as the actors age in this three-volume spectacle wherein the fastest gay drummer in the world finds God, where Gary the shouter hits the high seas like Odysseus, and where Hated Eric, one of the last remaining unsung superheroes of obscure punk history, gets a bit of airtime. What follows is part one of the trilogy and, as for me in this runtish history, I'm the guy putting it together. I was the guitarist for Hated Youth. Howdy. My name is John.

1.

Walking Down Freak Hill

FLYERS IN THE HALLS said boys who smoked pot grew breasts, so I checked my chest in the mirror. Didn't see any breasts hanging off the front of my body, but my eyeballs looked sunken down into my skull. The skin around my eyeballs looked thin and dark. That was from the smoke I sucked into my lungs each morning up on Freak Hill before classes began. At lunch I puffed away too, sometimes going off into the kudzu with my freak pal Lizard to watch freights rumble by along the tracks. One afternoon in English, the teacher walked over to my desk at the back of the room. She bent at the waist to look in my eyes. She said, "John, are you stoned?" I mumbled something. She said, "Go to the office and wait for me there." I started to leave, but, "No," she said, "I'm going with you," at which point I dashed into the hall. I heard her heels coming after me on the polished floor, and bolted down the stairs, tossed my sack of weed into the janitor's chill space then walked on to the principal's office where I sat and waited for the folks who ran shit to decide what to do with me. While sitting there I reached into my pocket without being seen by the secretaries. I grabbed my pipe and stuffed it down my pants into my underwear.

My mom was called in from work. She met with Jack Gaskins, the vice principal of Leon High, then drove me home, but I hated that place. Had somebody burned it to the ground I would have been happy. Had somebody planted a bomb there and the whole school been blown to smithereens, along with most of the people inside it, I would have been pleased. Or so I told myself. The school was crushing me. It even looked like a high security prison at the top of a hill. I was written referrals there. I did my hours of in-school suspension there. My science teacher smacked me on the back of the hand with a ruler there, but I always managed to get stoned in the mornings.

Freak Hill was on the other side of Meridian Road at the western edge of the campus where a short flight of concrete steps took you up to a vacant lot. Here longhaired guys in jeans jackets smoked bowls while sitting on makeshift seats or passed joints around a steel barrel that on cold mornings was stoked up with a fire. There was laughter and talking and a tall Black dude known as Roberto each morning sold machine-rolled peeners out of a zippered pouch, a dollar apiece, a seed rolled into the deal on each end. Whenever you lit one of Roberto's peeners, there was a pop and small explosion of sparks from the seed burning up and combusting. The hollows of my eyes deepened. The dark looked permanently inked into the hollows.

The hatred was mutual. The school wanted me gone, so gaining entrance into SOAR, the School of Analytical Reasoning where the stoner kids went, the hippie kids and Leon County's rejects and misfits—the brains, pregnant girls, rednecks and freaks—was the ideal fix. SOAR was your stoner kid's paradise. We passed joints around the fire barrel in the schoolyard and in the cemetery beyond the fence. We toked between classes, and now, instead of walking down Freak Hill to get to school, I moseyed down from the quiet cemetery.

Then Eric, the punk rocker from San Jose, California, moved to Florida. I'm pretty sure Eric was the first true punk to live in Tallahassee. Eric shared his music, cut my long hair off, and turned me into an aloof yet self-confident beast. We formed a band called the Little Johnnys. After doing two shows Eric decided our name was too gay. Our new and improved name was Hated Youth.

But that's getting ahead of myself.

Let's slow down, put things in sequence if we can.

I had been at SOAR several months when Eric entered eleventh grade in the middle of the term. I was in ninth grade, but since enrollment for the whole school was capped at 100 students, and this included grades seven and eight as well as the high school grades, students from different grades often took classes together, especially in courses like Art, Physical Education, and Music. Because of this, Eric and I had Music together. Before I even saw the guy, I heard him talking while I passed through the interconnected classrooms on my way to the music room after lunch. His voice was commanding, commandeering, loud, blisteringly confident. Whoever was attached to the voice, that person knew what he was talking about. When I stepped through the doorway, seeing him for the first time, I felt that I was encountering something special, that here was a force unlike anything I had so far encountered. Though only two years older than me, Eric could not be called a kid. He was his own person, in charge of himself, and also in charge, I would soon find out, of his French mom who drove him to and from school and often delivered him fat joints during lunch or between classes.

Eric was muscular but not freakishly so. A woman seeing him without his shirt on from across the street would probably have said he had beautiful arms. He was strong, his hair buzzed close on the sides of his skull and up top his hair was shorn short. That alone was different, especially since it soon became clear that Eric was anything but a square, that he was a bigtime pot smoker with a vast musical knowledge. Within minutes of being in the same room with this European-looking Clark-Kentish rebel, I heard him reel off names like Killing Joke, the Buzzcocks, and Gang of Four, bands I had never heard of. As a longhaired stoner freak my band narrative was a shaggy wet dog of complacent misery, a misery I mistook for liberation: AC/DC, Led Zeppelin, Queen, and Lynyrd Skynyrd. That was about it. Eric wore tight jeans, a studded leather band around his wrist, and his shirt had the sleeves cut off. He presented an alternative to what I, in my ignorance, viewed as the only pathway to cool.

I was just learning to play guitar. I played "Sweet Home Alabama" for Eric, which he dismissed as juvenile, though he may have been impressed with my technical skill. He picked up one of the guitars and with a pick started pounding on the E string. He dropped his index finger onto the G note and hit it four times. Back and forth he went from the open E to the pressed G. I joined what he was doing with the two-note version of bar chords and already we had a song going. That's all it took, two notes done over and over, back and forth. Eric even sang something, nothing I ever would have imagined being in a song—it was random, nothing anybody would think about if they were to think about "singing." I felt exhilarated. I couldn't wait to do it again.

Within days Eric's mom, who zipped around in a light blue Volkswagen Bug, was driving us from school out to a house in the Velda Dairy neighborhood north of the city. Here Eric lived in a garage-turned-into-a-room at the bottom of a crushed stone driveway. This one-room house of its own sat beside his parents' big house of wood. Eric's room had a bed, a dresser, a few chairs, but what gave the room its distinction was the state-of-the-art Bang & Olufsen turntable, the pair of Bose 901 Series IV stereo speakers, and Eric's massive record collection, all this cool shit like Black Flag, Jody Foster's Army, Circle Jerks, Dead Kennedys and the Sex Pistols. Then there was all this other cool shit Eric had that was more in the way of New Wave, bands with names like Random Hold, Tuxedo Moon, Joy Division, Depeche Mode and Our Daughter's Wedding who sang a great one that went, "Lawn chairs are everywhere, they're everywhere, my mind describes them to me." It was catchy, but what made me love it more was the way Eric sang along with it, running his arm out as though scanning the horizon while surfing.

I'd never met anybody so into music. We would sit for hours in his room listening to record after record and smoking joints. Eric quickly bought a bass guitar. As I already had an electric imitation SG that I played through a Peavey amp, we started putting songs together, sometimes breaking open a few Black Beauty pills and snorting up the powder that came out of them. It would grow dark and Eric's mom, God bless her, would drive me back to my house in Waverly Hills.

I had always been a nobody. Maybe nobody's not the best word. A problem I had had at my last school was the bullying. If I am in any way a testament to the nature of bullying, it follows you. When you transfer from elementary school into middle school, the bullying gets worse. Then you enter high school, and it flies over the top. Identifying the strange kids and being mean to them was the cool thing to do, and everybody wanted a piece of the action, even the weird kids themselves sometimes, and the teachers too. Sometimes I fought back and got in trouble but mostly I went with the flow, like the time this huge sort of rednecky character who loved trying to make me look ridiculous plunked somebody's astronomy project, a cardboard dome featuring the location of the stars on the inside, over my head. To be funny, I turned my head around as though I suddenly saw something I'd never seen before and was amazed. The whole class laughed. The guy slapped the cardboard "hat" off my head and that's when the teacher walked in. He saw that I had been causing a disturbance and so made me stand up and look at the cinder block wall for the rest of the class period.

I didn't want to be there. It was the theme of my high school experience until I entered SOAR, where teachers went by their first names, and where I met Eric who made me feel valuable for the first time in my life. Years later I would learn that this is a thing narcissists do, make you feel special to build up power over you, knowing all the while, as they do it, that you crave acceptance and validation. They know if they hold back on the attention they give, suddenly you'll be back in Nobody City. But again, "nobody's" not the word. As an oddball and therefore target for anybody who wanted to build themselves up at another's expense, I filled a role in a hierarchical design. Was anything built without somebody or other getting screwed along the way? The screwing of somebody was, so it seemed, necessary for anything to be built. It was a condition of progress.

Eric made me feel powerful. Subdued maybe but powerful and like I mattered, like I could separate myself from the stuff in life that sucked: the jocks, the parents, the encroaching responsibilities. When Eric cut off my hair one night at his place north of town, cutting it down to something more like his, I saw myself in the mirror as a whole new person. I ran through the moonlight in front of his house, on speed, and felt for the first time the power of self-determination. How could I have gone my whole life with the same stupid bowl-style haircut? I was new. My responsibility was to myself, and part of this responsibility meant not thinking about responsibility. Like this I looked better. Even the zits now visible on my forehead were beautiful compared to that thick brown curtain of hair. Running along Apollo Trail that night under the stars in front of Eric's house, I felt great joy, the blood all rushing fast in my veins. I knew a change had taken place in my life, one sure to determine everything that followed.

2.

Enter Lucia; and Getting a Band Together

NOW THERE WAS A BIG-LIPPED GIRL at SOAR in 1981 who went around in tight jeans and espadrilles. She happened to be dating the college-aged drummer for the Slut Boys, a band later described in a 1999 issue of *The Oxford American* as "The Greatest Garage Band Ever." Lucia wrote poetry. She claimed to have read every book in the school library. I believed her. Like Eric, she was her own person. Like Eric, she loved getting high. One day at lunch we three went into the graveyard. We ducked through some flowering azalea bushes into an organic dome, sitting room only, where we lit up some great sinsemilla, oh how it kills'ya. The smoke drifted between our faces. Soon we were high, sprinkled with flowery shadows that shifted around on our skin as we moved, Lucia saying somebody in California had addressed a letter to "Hippy High School" in

Tallahassee. The letter arrived at SOAR even though no street address was written on the envelope. What a laugh.

Lucia said her favorite place to get high was in her boyfriend's house on the other side of the graveyard where all these glass windows looked out into the Oakland Cemetery. The light would come in through the windows and make the objects in the room shine in a holy kind of way. If she was alone, which she liked best, she could look out the windows at the gravestones and write poetry. She liked the free, peaceful feeling that came over her when she got stoned and she liked the way smoke looked drifting around the light-filled room.

It was nice there under the dome, our walls dotted with pink blooms.

Three though, as opposed to the regular two, the Eric-and-I I was used to, felt awkward. Lucia wore a dark green fluted tank top, and it was clear she had no bra on. As we sat there stoned, eye whites glossy and pink, Eric said, "Nice shirt," and Lucia looked down. "Thanks," she said. She pulled out the bottom hem as though to show us the shirt better, then slowly let go, the elastic fabric settling back around her breasts, cradling them.

This moment brought Eric and Lucia together. It didn't matter that she lived on the other side of the graveyard with the Slut Boy who, as Lucia said, made her dress him in the morning, put his shoes on for him and all that. She would fix him breakfast and get him out the door so he could cut lamb at some Greek place at the Governor's Square Mall. What mattered was Eric was into her, and Lucia was into Eric. They were the same age, both Scorpios.

They were destined to become a couple.

In the meantime, Eric and I worked on putting a band together. After the school year ended, Eric bought his first car, a small white boxy Renault 10. Across its hood he spray-painted VOITURE in black. One day driving along Thomasville Road on our way out to the band room, we saw this tall skinny guy, a bit haggard and dirty-looking, walking along the side of the road, a little bit hunch-backed, a guy at least ten years older than us. Eric pulled over. He ran over to the guy and asked if he wanted to be the singer of a band. The guy said sure and, even though he'd been walking the opposite direction, he got in Le Voiture with us and we drove out to the band room and played together, the guy nice and weird with an interesting look. Coming up with words on the spot, he sang, "There once was a shoe, there once was a shoe, there once was a shoe and it didn't like you."

Now all we needed was a drummer. One day pulling into Wendy's for some of those awesome hamburgers with the square-shaped patties, we noticed this green Honda hatchback packed with drums. When we arrived at the pickup window, Eric asked the guy who handed us the bag of burgers whose car that was. The guy said it was his car. "Would you like to play drums with us?" Eric asked. "Sure," the guy said, and when his shift ended he drove out to the band room north of town.

He was David, on the chubby side with zits and he sweat a lot and had a perpetual smell of hamburger grease from working at Wendy's and eating the free burgers allowed to employees. He had just graduated from Godby

High School, so was a few years older than us, but man could David play. That first day, feeling exhilarated by how well we clicked, we walked up to the end of the driveway and were talking. One of Eric's neighbors came jogging along, and David said, almost like it was a song, "Jog off the fat, jog off the fat, ha ha haaa!"

Eric and I didn't think twice about do we or don't we want David. There was no need to talk of it. David was our drummer.

As for the tall hunchbacked guy, he was a good singer but not aggressive. He was good for jamming with in a Joy Division or Flipper kind of way, both excellent bands, but he didn't push limits. He was weird, looked cool and was mysterious. He would've made a great avant-garde artist of some sort. What he wasn't was hyperactive and angry and chaotic. He did not have the frenzied and impactful energy of Darby Crash from the Germs or Henry Rollins from Black Flag. Though we may not have known precisely what we were after, we felt the need for a powerful belt of angst and outrage, a sound of broken leashes and approaching danger. We were not sold on our singer.

The summer of 1981 ended. The new school year began, though Eric and Lucia did not return to continue their fun studies at SOAR. At some point this guy Gary who I remembered from the seventh grade entered SOAR. This happened a month or so after school started, which meant Gary wasn't wanted by the larger culture. Gary was another of Santa's misfit toys, and as such welcomed by the School of Analytical Reasoning.

During Phys. Ed. one day Gary and I were in a tree,

talking music at the edge of the softball field where our classmates ran around the bases in the sunshine, slamming balls with bats. Before transferring to SOAR, Gary said, he'd seen me once running up the sidewalk with my electric guitar case in front of Leon High. He'd been like *Who's that guy with the long-sleeved button-up shirt with stuff spray-painted all over it? He seems like he's involved in something different and cool.* After realizing I was John, that kid from seventh grade, he felt excited over the notion that he too could be a person who broke the mold. Gary could be different if he wanted, and Gary had already heard the Sex Pistols on WFSU, the college radio station. Gary loved that shit. Gary wanted to be a part of a scene, so when I asked Gary if he wanted to try out for the band, Gary said, "Hell yes!"

Eric came to pick me up that day from school in Le Voiture, and I introduced him to Gary. We drove Gary out to the band room and that very first day that all four of us were together—Eric, David, Gary and me—we put together "Hardcore Rules," our trademark song that exploded as if from a void at breakneck speed, impossibly fast and buzzy with shouts rife with joy and desire, an inexorable wall built of everything we had inside—this was everything we had to give—all this bottled-up angst and hatred for stuff we didn't like or understand. As Darby Crash would have had it, we were "puzzled panthers" who'd come into this world without rhyme or reason. We knew not why we were here but sensed that we were caged and that more cages waited for us later. In the fight against this abstraction, we poured our energy into this song that began with a few lines David wrote down on a hamburger receipt: "I wanna join the IRA, kill off one or two someday, I wanna be a terrorist, I wanna be an anarchist."

It was fast, it could not be faster, and the lead I did for it was a high-pitched water-dribble down a drainpipe into a river of distortion. The song was so fast that it ended almost before you had a chance to notice it started. We worked on the song. Instead of counting the song off with drumstick clicks or a shouted "one two three four," Eric shouted, "My name is God. Fuck you!" That's when the song started. In addition to wanting to join the IRA, God also, as revealed in the next verse, wanted to "join the KKK," and "kill off the minority." God wanted to "be the president," because maybe then he could pay his rent. The song's refrain was: "Hardcore rules, no more cool, hardcore rules, we need more hardcore." We were a hardcore band, strictly American, and we lickety-split put a set together.

Our first show, as the Little Johnnys, was at Daniel's Hair Salon in downtown Tallahassee. Daniel was an older brother of Eric's. Eric had quite a few brothers, as a matter of fact. In addition to Daniel there was Alain, Eric's younger brother, and Clark who still lived in San Jose and was guitarist for a band called Thieves' Cross. Eric had several more brothers in France, and also a sister, though those had been made with a different father. Only three or four folks attended our first show, *if that*, but it was a start. We later arranged to play in the gym at SOAR, where a good portion of the school, numbered at about a hundred, were in attendance. It was the first time I had been a cynosure in a positive way, and it felt great. Eric and I had mohawks now. All eyes were on us. With Gary and David we owned the floor with our chords and amps and reverberations. Something was happening to me. This being-seen thing was new and wonderful and gave meaning to my general disposition of being alone. We were making noise, our noise, and people were here to listen to us.

Our first *real* show was in July, almost a full month after Israel invaded Lebanon, an event I cared nothing about. It was *in the news* is all, Bob Schieffer and Dan Rather reporting, a bona fide war that would last in those faraway "biblical" regions until 1985, bombings and massacres included. The show happened outside on the campus of Florida State University at what they called the Union Green, Eric unstoppably arrogant in a sleeveless t-shirt with I HATE PEOPLE spray-painted on it. Between songs, Eric said stuff that lauded Ronald Reagan, stuff that sexualized women, and stuff that some of our audience of about 200 people were sure to take as anti-gay.

People came up to congratulate us afterwards, saying they'd never seen anything so fast. Somebody even complimented me on my guitar playing, which I took as a great surprise. Five days later, on July 8, 1982, a review of the show appeared in the college paper, *The Florida Flambeau*. Of us, somebody called Rick Revco, a writer moonlighting from the *Tallahassee Democrat*—his real name was later revealed as Steve Dollar—wrote: "Hawked and skinned, Tally's teenage version of the Dead Kennedys succeeded in making people hate them, or show affection by slam-bashing placid spectators. Bassist Eric likes to cuss a lot, using arrogance as a pose, while singer Gary leans into his mike screaming and stuttering to keep up with the manic beat (really "Nazi Punks Fuck Off" in doubletime?). It's all effective visually and aurally. Good nasty fun."

Dollar titled his Revco article, "Has nouveau punk hit Tallahassee?" A photographer from the paper shot us wedged into a narrow space between the old Floridan Hotel, soon to be demolished, and another building downtown. The picture appeared alongside the article in a goulash of news including a report on the progress of Operation Peaceful Galilee—"Will Israel reap the whirlwind?"—a declaration by Vietnam to "withdraw a significant number of its 200,000 occupational troops from Cambodia," and the number of rapes on women in Tallahassee so far this year: 35.

Gary zeroed in on Dollar's line about us succeeding to make people hate us. Gary wasn't much fond of the name, the Little Johnnys. Like what was that about? Nobody knew save Eric who would say, "Trust me, it's cool." The notion of being hated was cooler, so let's call ourselves Hated Youth! These changes were all in the way of "finding ourselves," a thing every adolescent goes through in the search for—*ugh, am I really going to say this?*—identity. We were young, we were hated, we liked being hated.

3.

Diane Arbus Plus a Thing About School

BEFORE HATED YOUTH, before the Little Johnnys, when Eric and I pounded stuff out together at SOAR, just the two of us, we tried some names on for size. Our first was the Rubber Nipples. After school we'd head out to Velda Dairy and experiment artsy-fartsy style in Eric's room, recording unplanned stuff on cassette tapes, Eric's little brother Alain sometimes joining in on sax while this guy Paul did drums.

I learned how to play "California Über Alles" by Dead Kennedys and "Where's Captain Kirk?" by Spizzenergi. Our stuff started getting faster, naturally, and Eric often complained that he could not make the bass do what he wanted it to do. Playing well and getting better took dedication, practice. Eric had other interests: girls, French cars, smoking weed, bench-pressing weights, looking cool.

The name "Rubber Nipples" was nothing I would or could have come up with. It was Eric's idea start to finish, and maybe it was funny? You couldn't expect milk to come out of a rubber nipple, could you? Was that what life was? A false promise? No satiation forthcoming? "Nipples" was a weird word, and maybe not a very likeable word. I did not even think of guys as having nipples. From my point of view, only girls had them and the only girl I ever was around was this Lucia character who'd dropped out of nowhere into our mix.

One day at SOAR, on a rare occasion when Lucia and I were in the music room alone, Lucia busted out an LP she wanted me to know about. She pulled the black disk reverently from its sleeve and set it on the school's portable turntable. It spun around and she placed the needle at the track she wanted me to hear. It was the Ramones doing, "Do You Wanna Dance?" This music Lucia held up high like something I should get into. It was the first time I'd heard the Ramones, and I thought it was awful. I was confused by what Lucia saw in the lyrics and slow repetitive iteration by the singer of "Do you wanna dance?" My answer to the question was no, I didn't want to dance, not that kind of dance, and especially not in the "moonlight" with the guy singing the song—how ridiculous. It wasn't even their own song. I had heard it on the golden oldies station, and even the Beach Boys did a version of it. In vain Lucia told me why this music was great. She started moving her shoulders to the beat, then danced to it, a kind of sock hop that to me, then, was lame.

When it was over Lucia put the Ramones record back in its sleeve. I think it was the boyfriend's record, the one who lived above the graveyard who, as he would tell me forty years later, "used to fuck her on those marble slabs at night." Through him Lucia had entered Tallahassee's alternative music scene, transforming from a redneckish type who'd been in a Woolco fashion show in 1973 at the Tallahassee mall to a brainy punk rock girl. Lucia had brought the Ramones record down through the gravestones to school and had played it special for me. Now I knew who the Ramones were. I wasn't impressed.

Back then, even as Rubber Nipples, Eric and I felt guided by the new American sounds on the 1981 compilation album, *Let Them Eat Jellybeans!* Could we do something similar? The Dead Kennedys, Black Flag and Circle Jerks were the best thing out there, the Bad Brains track and all of the bands resonating with rebellion and a dismissal of the "system." In 1979 the Germs had released *GI*, the LP with a beautiful blue circle offset in a square of black. JFA appeared in '81, as did LA's Wasted Youth whose album *Reagan's In* hinted that we were on the cusp of an explosion of hardcore bands whose records would be coming out over the next two and three years.

By the time the semester ended Eric and Lucia could be seen walking around SOAR's campus holding hands and looking punk. This pissed off Lucia's Slut Boy boyfriend who liked having a girl in the house put his clothes on for him, a girl who did other things, too. He wasn't prepared to let her go. When she broke it to him that she was with Eric, he got a little nutty. Lucia ran away from him. She needed a place to go, a new place to be, so started living in Eric's room north of town.

Over the summer Eric and I hung out and played in the Velda Dairy band room, and often Lucia was there with all these great books she'd checked out from the FSU library on a friend's card. One was the Diane Arbus classic called *Diane Arbus*. On its front cover was a photo of identical twins in raincoats looking spooky. Open the book, you saw people being themselves, all of them off in some way. One photo showed a shirtless dwarf on a bed near a bottle of booze, another had in it a hunchbacked giant towering over his normal-sized parents. Not only that, but the giant, as revealed in the point-blank title, was Jewish. You've probably seen the book, so I don't need to speak of its content, but those photos gave me a hollowed-out feeling of quiet amazement. The secrets were here, exposed. One guy, naked and pale, concealed his weenie between his legs so that he looked like a woman. There was the close-up of the child crying, one of my favorites, and then, of course, the photo of the little boy in Central Park holding a plastic hand grenade, an image Hated Youth would soon use on a flyer. "This photo says everything there is to say," Lucia said, and told me how the photographer one day climbed into a bathtub and slit her wrists with a razor blade. What?

Lucia was two and something years older than me and had somehow acquired a car. She came and went at the band room as she pleased. One day, while Lucia was in the main house with Eric's mom who liked to juice stuff—carrots and beets and things that were healthy—Eric picked up the long white vibrator I had seen lying around since before the time Lucia entered our lives. It was the kind of vibrator meant for sticking *into* a body as opposed to *onto* a body. It was about a foot long, the circumference of a zucchini you might find in Publix, and ridged along the trunk. While Lucia was in the house, Eric said sometimes he would come into the room to find her on the bed on her back, legs up wide and the thing inside her going. He marked with his thumbnail how far in she could take it. He smelled it, then offered it to me for a smell. I respectfully declined.

When Lucia came back into the room I had to picture her speared by the white battery-operated object. Through Eric's description I had looked into her life, had taken a sneak peek at her in the same way people did the subjects of Diane Arbus. It was an invasion of privacy, but knowing Eric meant you had to know such things. He was a great storyteller. He loved telling the one about how he saw the Plasmatics perform in California, how Wendy-O "worked her cunt up into a froth" on the corner of a guitar amp. Another of his stories took place in France when he and some guys grabbed a woman in jeans off the street and drove her into the countryside. As the woman struggled and they restrained her, the driver of the car plowed straight into a cornfield. "The corn was slapping against the windshield like this!" Eric said with great excitement and made the noise of corn stalks slamming a car's windshield, hand and arm gestures included. The woman's clothes had about been ripped off by the time the driver stopped the car, at which point they dragged the woman outside, placed her on the hood and proceeded to fuck her. That may have been where the story ended. I don't remember Eric saying if they left the woman in the cornfield, or if they let her put her clothes back on or what. For all I knew the story could have been true, or maybe Eric was embellishing on something he'd heard somebody else say, or had seen in a movie. He did talk appreciatively, sometimes, after all, about the rape scenes in *A Clockwork Orange*. I didn't ask questions. I did not think about it much then, or later. It simply was one of many stories Eric now and then told.

Eric also liked sticking his finger in Lucia's mouth. She would hold it with her fat lips and he would remove it slowly. As with his raunchy, sometimes violent stories, I showed almost no interest. I put those things in a box in my mind somewhere, closing them away. But he liked me to watch. He would walk her around the room by the pussy. Make her go this way or that way. Or connect both hands together between her legs, one side to the other, and turn his body as though he were the column in the middle of a carrousel. While he rotated, Lucia stepping mincingly, he made carrousel music sounds, Lucia one of the painted animals kids rode round in circles on. Like Eric, Lucia was proud of her rejection of underwear. If wearing no underwear wasn't cool, what was? There seemed always to be a sizeable gash, what people called a camel toe, between Lucia's legs, and now, as a fiberglass carnival object, said camel toe served as the socket for a ball joint.

One day that summer of '81, or night I guess I should say, Eric and Lucia came over to my house excited over this book they had called *In Watermelon Sugar*, a book whose cover featured a black and white photo of a guy who looked like Meathead from *All in the Family*, the author, I presumed.

In front of him and to his side, a woman in a skimpy hippy dress looked off sideways while the guy looked into the lens.

It was different, and though Eric acted like the book was his discovery, I knew it wasn't. It was a Lucia thing whose coolness Eric had picked up on. In watermelon sugar? How amazing was that? The incantatory quality of the first line had us marveling: "In watermelon sugar the deeds were done and done again as my life is done in watermelon sugar."

I loved it, and the name of its author, Richard Brautigan, would not be forgotten.

While in my room that night, talking about *In Watermelon Sugar*—and Lucia loaned me the book so I could read it—we discussed the logistics of a heist we'd had it in mind to commit: steal a desk-chair-combo, the old kind from the fifties made of steel and wood with a cubby hole for books and school supplies. I had mentioned that I knew where one was during a discussion that began after Lucia showed us a photo in a book of a woman wrapped up in leather bondage gear while tied, bent over, to a stepladder. In Le Voiture, Eric drove us a block over to Windsor Way. He took us two blocks up, slipped left onto Piedmont, drove down the hill and up the other side to Meridian Road, which happened to be an actual meridian like the kind you see on the globe. The Renault had this quality of revving as if the car was gaining speed, moving fast in a *here comes trouble* kind of way. The revving engine always announced Eric's approach. In this way, revvingly, we crossed Meridian Road onto the campus of the North Florida Christian School, which was for kids in the twelfth grade all the way down to kindergarten. Word from the trenches was now and then a teacher walked by your desk with a pencil. If you were a boy, the teacher stuck the pencil behind your ear and pulled out whatever hair you had tucked behind it. If the pencil trick revealed your hair as too long, you were sent home and not allowed back until you cut it. The girls, of course, had to have their skirts pan out below their knees. A few times, as an elementary school kid, I pedaled my bike up there on Sundays and during the televised service in the big church sat back and watched. That's how I learned of the three Hells, how the deepest Hell is the hottest, reserved for the worst sinners. The flames of the other two levels of Hell produced light, but in that deepest Hell all you saw was black.

Eric and Lucia wanted the desk-chair-combo so that Eric could tie her to it, bent over like the woman from the picture, and fuck her from behind.

Eric killed Le Voiture's engine in the service pass between the football field and church, and we hurried up the hill onto the porch of the old shack, once somebody's house, used as a storage space for the school. No flashlight. We stepped through the doorway into the pure black musty place of cobwebs and loose boards and felt around, grabbed one of the desk-chair-combos and ran it down the hill to Le Voiture. Those R10s are small cars. We tore out of there with me crammed into the back seat with the desk mashed against my face, digging into my ribs. Once back at my place we smoked a joint in the shaded area to the side of my house, by the pool pump where the aspidistra grew, and then they moved on with their desk-chair-combo, the revving of Le Voiture fading slowly, disappearing into the night.

Another time, driving along in Lucia's car, a sedan, Eric at the wheel, Eric shot us down the parking lot behind Montgomery Ward at the Tallahassee mall, Lucia's leg touching mine. Our legs kept brushing against each other. This was unusual and weird. In this manner Eric drove us into the Stoner Woods where we bumped along a dirt road through the trees. Eric parked us in one of the hideaway nicks where we hot-boxed it. Once we were stoned out of our minds, or at least I was, Eric pinched one of Lucia's breasts between his thumb and fingers. As before, her chest was covered over by fluted fabric, no bra. As Eric squeezed her tit, pinching it together into a misshapen lump, him with a smirky smile on his face, Lucia stared at me expressionlessly through bloodshot eyes, or perhaps there was a trace of expectancy on her mouth, a tiny smile there. "Let's tie her to a tree," Eric said.

Lucia nodded. "It's okay."

"That's what those ropes back there are for," Eric said.

"I don't know," I said. They were looking at me, waiting, taking delight, it seemed, in my awkward response to their proposal. They were waiting for me to say okay.

"There's this pile of garbage over there," I said. "I'm gonna go check it out," and I got out of the car. I went over to the place junk was piled up and looked around in the dumped stuff—weird pieces of metal, strange refuse that included a hijacked and plundered newspaper machine, its change box pried open with a crowbar. Who even knows what I was thinking, I was just in the junk looking around at stuff, trying not to think as I waited for them to finish whatever they were doing and call me back over.

Without getting out of the car, they finally called for me.

I don't know. The whole tits thing with Lucia may have unnerved me. Can't say, just titties do make inroads into the minds of teenaged boys, wherever they live. "Did you see her tits?" Eric said that first time we talked about Lucia behind her back. That was after we got stoned with her that first time in the cemetery next to SOAR. Eric said, "She basically said look at my tits. I looked right at them. Nice, right?" He slapped my arm with the back of his hand.

Oh, when hot girls walked by, Eric's head tilted, shifted, panned, his gaze soaking up all it could of the body parts covered in denim, silky fabrics or soft cotton. He would go, "botoooo," and flex his chops and wiggle his fingers. Those times he ran his finger in and out of Lucia's mouth, he'd say, "Isn't that beautiful, John?" and wait for me to nod my head, or provide some kind of acknowledgement that it was.

It may have been, beautiful. In retrospect it was. Then, though, it was too close, too real and in my face for me to pause and admire. So much easier to stare at an image in a "dirty" magazine where the woman is flat and made of paper, nonexistent, harmless. In these very woods, in fact, woods I knew well in that I'd walked through them a hundred times from my house in Waverly Hills to the Tallahassee mall, you now and then came across rain-damaged *Playboy* magazines that smelled of old sunshine and mold and left your fingers feeling slick and chemically. If you were lucky, you might stumble upon a stack of *Penthouse*, the hard stuff. The glossy pages were sometimes stuck together from being out in the changing weather. When you pulled them apart to see the next naked lady picture, the paper would rip. As you continued pulling back the pages you ended up with naked ladies of warped dimensions, women with body parts of other women stuck to them, double-headed three-eyed one-breasted five-legged monster women that despite their cubist dimensions did not fail to titillate.

I was being acculturated, and Eric was the trustworthy representative from the land of reason. This act of Eric pulling his index finger out of Lucia's mouth while she held it with her lips defined the nature of things, the saliva, the pulling out, the pushing in. The largeness of her lips and how they wrinkled up some as the finger withdrew was the perfect allusion to a mysterious act I had not yet committed.

Driving away from the Stoner Woods behind Montgomery Ward that day, Lucia's leg did not bump against my leg as it had, a short while ago, on the trip in. What a weird feeling. Her leg seemed to cringe from my leg. Was she mad at me? This sensation of being punished by a girl for not following along with her plan was a new shade in my experience of human interactions. She had seemed to like me and then suddenly she didn't like me. Did that make of her initial like a lie? Had I helped Eric tie her to a tree and gone along with whatever scenario they'd imagined, what then? It's the sort of thing that's driven people far and wide berserk and has made them do crazy things, things like drive their car at top speed into concrete walls, or smash someone they love in the face with a brick. Some folks are more prone to getting emotionally crushed than others, sure, but in the gesture of Lucia's withdrawal were unseen horrors that only my future could reveal.

At the close of the summer of '81, on August 10, the weirdo kids and hippy girls and misfits from around Leon County returned to SOAR looking forward to a funtime repeat of the previous year. That's how it went at SOAR. Nearly every day of the week we took field trips to museums and parks and in class watched movies, learned of lysosomes and did our math. In Social Studies we watched every episode of Alex Haley's *Roots*. We could goof around and act crazy without the sense that some higher authority was waiting to crush us. It was easy to tell that the teachers were good people. Though they reprimanded us from time to time, as they should have, and made occasional allowances that teachers at other schools would surely have frowned upon, they had our best interests in mind. So it was strange, a little, to see Eric bail on the first day of classes.

What I understood was this: a teacher at SOAR, the previous school year, had been smitten by Lucia's poetry. He'd been blown away, too, by what he thought was Eric's poetry. He asked if he could publish their poetry and they said yes, Eric never thinking that the teacher would actually go ahead and do it. During the summer, after the journal the teacher edited was released, somebody pointed out that the awesome poem published under Eric's name was really by Johnny Lydon, the Sex Pistols guy! It was on an album by Public Image Ltd. Eric had loved reciting the poem in an English accent, which had one day caught the teacher's attention. The teacher was like, "Wow, did you write that?"

and Eric, feeling lifted up by the positive attention, said, "Yeah."

The shit embarrassed the shit out of the teacher, or maybe he'd felt more hurt by the lie. He demanded a conference. The conference didn't go well. I just remember Eric getting back into the light blue Bug with his mom on the first day of school and the two of them leaving campus. In my mind I was like *Wait, where are you guys going?* Though Eric blew it off as insignificant, telling himself, and us, that he had better things to do than attend some bullshit fucking school, the moment would have a major impact on his life. Instead of taking the road to the fork where advanced education might have been a choice, he dug his kicks into Manual Labor Lane. Nine days later he handcuffed himself to Lucia. Locked at the wrist, they watched the Psychedelic Furs play at Tommy's Deep South Music Hall on Tennessee Street.

4.

When We Were the Stink Cracks

IN DECEMBER '81, after changing our name from Rubber Nipples to Pluto to Stink Cracks, Eric rented an empty storefront off the "old Negro strip" on Macomb Street across from the newly constructed Civic Center, a stadium-style building hosting indoor shows with unlimited seating, the first of its kind in Tallahassee. Our one-room rehearsal space shared a wall with the rehearsal space of the Slut Boys, their space known by musical showgoers and scenesters as the OK Club. People went there late at night to dance and party and listen to real music played by the coolest kids in town. The walls of the OK Club were draped in an old parachute. There were amps in there and liquor bottles, broken guitar strings and ashtrays, all sorts of fun stuff that said you were in the presence of small-town musical gods. I wanted to join in, but the arrangement of us and the Slut Boys side by side garnered negative vibes from the Slut Boys.

Why? Well, other than sharing a wall with a younger generation whose music could be heard reverberating in their own space, Eric had stolen their drummer's teenaged sex partner, had pulled that girlfriend-rug out from under him like some kind of nasty magic trick. Lucia's ex was nonplussed as hell about it. He was, after all, the guy Lucia had painted up as a bad boy, turning him into a kind of untouchable legend. In his dark shades and cool leather jacket that Eric said must've been sandblasted to get so supple, Donny struck the figure of a dangerous renegade. But he was popular. Lucia told us how he would press a victory-v sign against his face so that his mouth was cradled in the crotch between those two fingers. Driving along in his car through the sunshine he would look out his window at cute college girls and stick his tongue out, flicking his tongue over the webby space where the girl's pussy would be were his fingers her legs.

At that time, before we had evolved into the Little Johnnys, our drummer was Paul, a kid who, like me, went to SOAR. Paul's dad had been some kind of genius in the world of Jazz drummers, and Paul took after his dad with delayed hits and wildly rolling tumbles. Paul's style gave me the sense that he was barely hanging on, though he played impressively fast. In our new practice space, Eric, Lucia and I started developing a set in yet another band we were calling Vinyl Punks. While Lucia sang her own lyrics mixed up with shrieks and moans, strumming made-up chords on my guitar, I played Eric's bass, Eric banging the drums.

One day while Vinyl Punks were playing a song, Lucia's Slut Boy ex shouted something out there on the sidewalk. He threw a beer bottle against our door where it met with the floor. Glass shards slid over the threshold into our band room. Eric threw down his sticks and ran out there. We heard shouting, some kind of confrontation going on. A few seconds later Eric rushed back inside, grabbed his sticks, got back behind the drums and started pounding while shouting, "Neil Young gave me head! Neil Young gave me head!"

To the Slut Boys we may have posed a threat. From what I understood, the Slut Boys had some originals, but mostly they played repeats from other bands. It was one more reason why the OK Club was popular. Folks loved to come around and hear their trusty faves, songs like "Louie Louie" and "Born to be Wild" and "God Save the Queen." As things were, the Slut Boys, who'd played with Joan Jett and Iggy Pop at Tommy's on Tennessee Street, along with a multi-gendered new wave punk band called the Implications, also from Tallahassee, held the Heavy Weight Punk Champion Belt in Tallahassee. They had been the ones pushing the envelope, and even U2 had come down to their OK Club to jam with them, so what was up with all this noisy crap going on next door?

We had rented the space fair and square, so this guy Donny could go have whatever hissy fit he wanted. Our interest was in making music, and this new band we were doing with Lucia singing poetically and hypnotically, as much of a slap in the face or heartbreak or whatever else it may have been for Donny, was just getting started.

For me, playing bass was great fun, I loved it, that was the end of it. It hardly mattered what was going on around me, what other musicians were doing, it could be anything so long as I had permission to play some simple line over and over. I liked getting lost in the physicality of it. I liked the way the fat strings of the bass felt sliding under my fingertips. I liked being the backbone, the trusted fulcrum or capstone without which the other sounds might wander aimlessly and be lost.

The discordant chords Lucia played were made up spidery combos of notes pressed into a chaos of open strings, chords she remembered, miraculously, and repeated while singing of big topics: death row, loneliness, aging, all this death and darkness. She sang as though her heart was clutched by some invisible force whose mandate was if you don't unload, I will squeeze tighter.

Though she'd not been taught how to sing, Lucia swiveled between deep throat sounds and high-pitched frantic screeches. Years later I would see how Lucia, like all great artists, understood the meaning of contrast, how to use opposites. As it was for all of us those days, she did not have to try hard to be good. She simply did what made sense, and it *was* good. In her singing hints of Johnny Rotten, of British influence, could be heard, but more likely than not such inflections were homage. Of all of the bands to come out of Tallahassee, nothing moves me more now, forty years later, than the three extant recordings of songs whose lyrics Lucia wrote and sang. They say Exene Cervenka from X went to FSU, and maybe Jim Morrison had ties to Tallahassee, as if this gives the town musical clout—so what! Lucia had them beat. Her song that I remember most from that time went: "Where were you when the lights went out? Were you thinking about me, were you thinking about me?" It was all so somber, so melancholy, so haunting.

A few times, between songs, Eric ran down the hall to the communal bathroom, shared with the Slut Boys. He'd jump back into the room a minute later and say, "Sorry, I had to jack off."

On New Year's Eve, around midnight, Eric picked Paul up from his mom's place in Killearn Estates, then drove into Waverly Hills for me. It still was 1981 when I climbed into Le Voiture. We drove out to our new practice space to work on our stuff for the Stink Cracks. An hour into 1982 we started playing. We got through one song. It sounded great, but right then Paul says, "I'm done. I need to get back home."

"What? What the fuck are you talking about, Paul? We just got here."

"I'm tired, take me home."

Making a declaration like this, to Eric, was the same as quitting.

"You know what?" Eric said, "Fuck you!" and grabbed up some of Paul's drums, took them outside and threw them into Macomb Street. Eric went back in for the rest of the kit and threw it all out there, Paul's crashing cymbals welcoming in the new year. Paul picked his drums out of the street, ordered them against the building and, hoping nobody would come along and steal them, went to the payphone at the Shell station around the corner to call his mother for a ride home.

5.

Hated Youth Plays Tennessee Street

OUR FIRST SHOW AS HATED YOUTH was at Tommy's Deep South Music Hall on Tennessee Street, the main drag running though Tallahassee east to west. On the same block with Tommy's was Bullwinkle's, a notorious college bar done up with wood pillars and railings to look like an old-time cowboy saloon, a place you might hitch a horse before mixing in with your drunken young lassies and athletic studs hanging out on the stoop. Also on Tennessee Street, atop the hill, was Asshole High, or *Leon*, the daytime human stockyard from which Gary and I escaped, finding our way to the School of Analytical Reasoning at the bottom of the hill in an area known as Frenchtown. That's where "the Blacks" lived. During lunch we SOAR kids rounded the corner to a place called Ferrell's Soul Food for biscuits and gravy.

Days prior to the show, Eric and Lucia and I walked up and down the strip with flyers we made, stapling them to the electrical poles on every intersection. We stapled them in front of Mike's Beer Barn, which sold liquor through a window on the back of the building, drive-thru style, 24 hours a day. We stapled them at the oddly shaped FSU Arts Building and by the TraveLodge whose red globes glowed only, Lucia said, when you could get a whore.

"Is there a future for Tallahassee's red-blooded sacrilegious punk scene?" Rick Revco wrote in the *Florida Flambeau* the month before. Answering his own question, he said, "Yes, but not on Tennessee Street." Revco ended the article with: "Support your favorite band and terrorize your neighborhood. Have a hardcore home party. It sure beats Phil Donahue."

The show at Tommy's was on August 12, 1982. The Know-It-Alls, a band popular with the college crowd, headlined, but also on the ticket was Hated Youth, the Speed Queens, Toxic Shock, and Grandma's House. Revco's prediction that Tennessee Street wasn't ready for us had proved false. Perhaps Revco was trying to work a bit of reverse psychology on the powers that be. Either way, the Little Johnnys, now Hated Youth, were *on the strip.*

We were too young to get into bars but arrangements had been made. My hair, newly cut, featured a mohawk with diagonal hair-crosses, bas-relief, on the sides, an unheard-of haircut, nothing anybody, as far as I knew, had ever been seen with in Tallahassee. Arriving at the show where a line of people stood to get in, I felt elevated. Nobody anywhere looked like me. I felt looked at and whispered about, but not in a bad way as it had been in the Leon County School system before I entered SOAR, the school that saved me. "Who's that guy?" people were saying. "He must be in one of the bands." I wore a long-sleeved white shirt that I had painted up with weird stuff, and jeans and sneakers.

Our time came. We took the stage. As it had been on the Union Green, we were on display before the thirsty eyes of showgoers. We and the other bands played our sets then watched the Know-It-Alls who were tight and did great choruses and sang artsy and technical for their fans.

Following the Tommy's extravaganza, *Democrat* staff writer Christopher Farrell, who happened to play bass for Speed Queens, and additionally jumped higher than any other dancer while doing the pogo at the local shows, began work on a sizeable article about the arrival of punk rock music in Tallahassee. Hated Youth and a handful of local punk rockers went to the newspaper building for a photoshoot. These "punks," myself among them, were photographed in different combinations and attitudes against a backdrop of random lines and shapes, an exuberant attempt made by somebody, the "art director," I would guess, to cross the styles of Lichtenstein with Basquiat, two artists popular and perhaps thought of as edgy at the time. "Make it look poppy and colorful and zingy and fresh with life!" the authority in charge may have said to her assistant, or newspaper intern, or janitor down the hall, whoever was on hand to lend their expertise in brushing differing colors of paint onto large sheets of paper. The full-page layout featured a photo of Eric in sleeveless shirt buttoned to the neck, collar turned up, flexing his bicep while making a hand shadow puppet. His mohawk was of the fluffy variety, not sharp due to the hair grown out on the sides. His mouth was opened wide as with a primal shout. The photo was inset against a checkerboard pattern, the overall effect being that Eric looked more artsy than scary, even a mite effeminate. In other photos on the same page kids were gathered together all smiling and looking harmless and happy and quaint and giggly. The attitude of this fun-loving grabby-armed family of punks was of root beer floats and pajama parties.

Farrell titled his article, "Young Punks: Restless Kids Stalk a New Style," and wrote it in tandem with another article directed at the parents of these unruly children, persuading them not to be too alarmed, that this was merely a part of the changing times. The companion article Farrell titled, "What Should You Expect When Your Son Comes Home With A Mohawk?" Both articles quoted the punks of the town, their responses to questions like, "Why do you do your hair like that?" and "Isn't there a lot of violence involved with punk rock?"

Not long after the articles appeared I was on my way to my neighborhood bus stop at Ivanhoe and Waverly, thinking I'd catch a bus to the Tallahassee mall instead of walking, as I normally did. A jeep chock-full of jocks pulled up beside me while I walked. The guy driving stopped the jeep. I paused. "You got any drugs?" one of the jocks up there asked. "No." Another jock coughed up a mogey and sent it flying my way. The glob of jock-snot hit my chest. In retaliation I cleared my throat, making it look like I was coughing something big up. I had in fact been eating Lays potato chips before they entered my world. From my mouth I sprayed the jocks in the jeep with a mixture of saliva and chip and went on my way.

A beefed-up jock dropped off the jeep to cajoling yips: "Knock him out, Bruck!" and "Come on, get 'im!" and here he came. Instead of taking off running, which may have been the wiser thing to do, I went towards him and started hitting as I had seen Eric hit when Eric told stories about hitting—fists forward, face back. Seemed like the way to go, and apparently it was a great strategy because the jock on the other end of my fists, the he-man guy whose intention it was to crush and humiliate all freaks, ended up in a head-lock that I happened to be administering. I saw myself leisurely pounding the guy's face. When I realized what I was doing, I let go, by which time he was bleeding from his mouth and nose. He stood up, the other jocks still coaxing him, but he backed away, got on the jeep and off they drove.

A Black woman dressed in white, somebody's maid in Waverly Hills—even her shoes were white—was standing at the bus stop. She had witnessed it all, and wanted no part of any of it. The bus came and we got on it. The bus moved out to Meridian Road and that's when I remembered that I *had*, actually, been knocked out. I touched the left side of my head. It was numb. I couldn't feel my temple at all, nor most of the left half of my scalp. That's where the jock smashed me sideways with his fist. What had happened, I gathered, was the jock knocked me into oblivion. I fell, but before hitting the ground, I came back to. That's when I jumped up and twisted the jock into a headlock and started smashing his face with my fist.

By the time the city bus let me off at the mall the pain in my brain was too much to handle. All I could do was agonize, but I managed to get a taxi home. I went in my house and got on my bed and did not get up until the next morning. For twenty years, and then thirty years, I would have nerve damage in my temple. The area was mostly numb and, strangely, I could scratch a spot on the right side of my head and an itch would start on my left temple.

That October '82, during the Extra Strength Tylenol cyanide poisoning scare, Farrell wrote a third article, this one for a competing paper, *The Florida Flambeau*, under the name Eddie Cochran. The article was titled, "The New Music Scene: Some Good, Some Bad," and in it Farrell/Cochran called his own band, the Speed Queens, "the most famous of Tallahassee's new bands, thanks to bass player Chris Farrell's music column for the *Tallahassee Democrat*." After lauding his own band in detail, Farrell, as Cochran, commented on the other emerging Tallahassee bands. "Hated Youth," Farrell wrote, "Is Tallahassee's genuine hardcore band, special because guitarist John Hodges was raised on a diet of methedrine and No-Doz." Then he said, "Bass player Eric Rodgers should consider an enema before he goes on stage. That might get rid of the crap he spews while performing. His antics, intending to be threatening but ending up limp and foolish, only interfere with the genuine intensity of singer Gary Strickland. And Hated Youth drummer David Whatshisname should consider losing half his kit."

After the article appeared, Farrell was fired by the *Tallahassee Democrat* for moonlighting, and Steve Dollar who'd done the article for the *Flambeau* using the name Rick Revco four months earlier in July, was fired on the same day. A colleague of Dollar and Farrell's at the *Flambeau*, after getting a call from an angry senior editor at the *Democrat*, ratted them out. Farrell made out well in the bargain, getting unemployment, but Dollar not so lucky. Though in the end the double firing served as an impetus for both writers to get the hell out of town, to each wend their way to a locale of greater action and opportunity—the Big Apple—for Dollar it was rough going at first. In his signature jacket, t-shirt, and hat, Dollar had to scrabble out a space for himself in the competitive field of writing about popular culture.

The *Democrat* may already have wanted to ditch Farrell in that Farrell was by nature outspoken, somewhat radical, and a tad on the touchy side. Even Nicky, my across-the-street neighbor who sold me the guitar I used with Hated Youth, a cheap-as-they-come imitation SG, knew about Farrell's touchy side, as Farrell had taken a course in English literature from Nicky's father, a professor at Florida State University. During one class, Nicky's dad made the claim that homosexual writers had an edge over heterosexual writers in that they were by nature more creative. Just look at Truman Capote who wrote *Breakfast at Tiffany's*, a book my friend's dad took as an American classic. Farrell, unabashedly gay, took issue. He stood up in class and duked it out verbally with the professor before storming off—that's what my buddy said went down in his father's course in Modern American Literature.

6.

Going Road Warrior

HATED YOUTH'S INCREDIBLE sweating drummer, not Domino Fats, but David Fats as we sometimes affectionately called David, knew the projectionist at the Miracle 5 movie theater. The projectionist would let David in for free and David would open the back door of the theater and the band, all of us with mohawks and shaved heads, would pile in to watch *Road Warrior*, which debuted in late December, 1981. Entering those hot sands of post-apocalyptic violence after band practice when we were all geared up on ourselves was a great fun thing we did together—our family time away from the band room. We identified with the anarchical crazies with mohawks and spikes and leather jackets who terrorized the upright citizens of the goody two-shoes community hoarding the gasoline. Eric especially identified with Lord Humungus's right-hand man, the scary guy with a red mohawk who jumped around like an animal screaming psychotically in chaps worn over bare flesh. Though much younger, Eric resembled the guy and in later years would come to embody not only this murderer's looks—really, they were the spitting image of each other—but the violent attitude, butting his head into peoples' heads in bars, knocking them out, getting into fights, looking scary, spreading fear and fucking all the girls. A badass. As for who I was in the movie that we watched seven times, eight times, nine times and more, the band agreed, it had to be the skinny weirdo seen flying through the desert in a gyrocopter, the one who gets his fingers chopped off when trying to catch a sharpened metal boomerang thrown by a dirty little desert child.

Being crazy had an allure.

One afternoon David and I were north of the city, rolling along through Eric's neighborhood in David's Hampstead green Honda hatchback when a blond girly-girl cut us off. David went after her, swinging a fat rusted chain outside the driver's window and screaming like one of the nutjobs from the movie. With my three hawks I leaned far out of the window and jabbered along with him. We followed this person down one street and another, swerving behind her, getting up on her tail like the Road Warriors do the goody two-shoes people, pretending like we were in the movie. I even had on my leather jacket that I got from Sears for 55 dollars, a huge investment that my mom fought me tooth and nail on. As David twirled the length of chain, now and then slamming its links against his car door, the threatening sound of metal on metal reaching the girly-girl's ears, causing her to pee her panties, we hoped, I sat up on the windowsill, deepening her panic. Was I to sidle onto the hood of David's car then jump onto her car like a true Road Warrior would? Sure seemed like it, and she kept checking the rearview mirror, slowing down a little then speeding up, even swerving out of her lane, smart girl, to prevent us from driving up alongside her. As she did not want us knowing where she lived, you can be sure she drove past her own house. She did not want us coming back later, after all, to wrap that chain around her girly neck. She may well have envisioned us yanking her out of the front door of her house into her yard, tearing her clothes off in the green grass then ripping her limb from limb. Whenever she turned down one street, David followed, revving that engine, almost ramming her until finally we said, "Fuck this shit," and hauled ass on over to the band room where we smoked a joint, listened to some records and turned on the amps.

My mom put me in the Chattahoochee ward, said I tried to hit her with a two-by-four! I didn't do a goddamn thing, she's the one who needs a shrink!

Though the anger in our songs was genuine, the line between actual violence and pretend violence was clear enough to me. Few things, in fact, could be more horrific than committing violence upon another person, but it was fun to act out, pretend you were dangerous while knowing it was a matter of choice as to whether or not you crossed that line. There was one time that I remember, when I was about nine, maybe ten, so many years before I'd even heard of Road Warriors, that I was sitting in the back of my dad's white Comet while he and my mother argued about something or other in the front seat. My dad's golf clubs were in the back with me, and I got to thinking I should kill them. I just hated them. Though I could not swing the golf club from the back seat, I somehow thought that I could accomplish this if I wanted, and it was like I was standing on one side of a thin hair stretched taut and about to break. When the hair broke, I would jump forward into my purpose of killing them—that's how detestable they were to me—smashing their heads with a club and causing them to bleed and *die die die!*

The notion of the line, the line that could be crossed like Ted Bundy crossed a line when he decided to end the life of a woman, and then more women with real blood pumping through their veins, was a thing I was aware of. Those women were completely real. They could be touched and real odors seeped from their bodies. Did fear have a smell?

As for Eric's relationship with violence and hatred, it seemed less insidious, more on the surface, was in plain view you might even say, and therefore predictable. Perhaps Eric was on the other side of "the line" already, and so grievances did not stew and build pressure such as they did with me and so many others. Eric's responses were not delayed. They played out in real time with little regard for potential consequences. To wit:

One night Eric and I wanted to get stoned but had no weed to speak of. We each had a few dollars, though, so we combined them for the magic number required to get a nickel bag. In Le Voiture we then headed over to Frenchtown. Crawling south along Macomb Street, we passed by the notorious Tropicana Lounge, the pool hall known as a place of danger, a place of prostitution, of drug dealings and weaponry. The place was exclusively Black.

We turned east onto West Virginia Street and stopped the R10 a little ways up from the intersection. A fellow hopped over from the other side of the street. "What'cha need? What'cha need?"

"Five," I said.

"You got it, cuz."

I gave him the bills and he gave me the 4"x3" manilla envelope that felt like it had some buds in there. Eric rolled on and we were glad to have scored, sort of bubbly with excitement. We had been worried a cop may have been lurking. So far so good. When we reached the stop sign at Martin Luther King Jr. Boulevard, we took a look at the weed. Turned out it was oregano. Eric floored it, circling—or rather squaring—the block. As we drove back up alongside the Tropicana he popped the R10 over the sidewalk down into a dirt parking area and jumped out. I jumped out after him, saying his name like *What're you doing? I don't think this is a great idea*, but Eric didn't care. I followed him across the street where the two of us burst through the front doors of the Tropicana. "Where is he, goddamnit?"

Brothers in suave clothes backed away from their pool tables, clutching their sticks and saying, "Yo. Yo," trying to figure out what was at hand, these two white kids in leather jackets with crazy fuck-ass *Injun* haircuts.

"The guy that sold me that fuckin' bogus bag of weed, where is he? I'm'a find him one way the other!"

The brothers remained confused, still trying to figure out the anomaly. They kept looking from us to each other then back at us with looks of alarm, confusion and indecision, a few of them leaving the club through the front and back doors.

The guy we were looking for was not in the club, not to be found in the bathroom either, so, "C'mon," Eric said and we went through the back door into the alley and looked for the guy there. The guy that had called us "cuz" had disappeared, so we went back to the car. That was both the first and last time I entered the Tropicana Lounge.

Another instance of Eric's fearlessness may show here:

Because the cops kept shutting Hated Youth down at our practice spaces, we sometimes hooked up with Sector 4 who had access, via their bass player's connections, to a place called Creative Preschool on the west side of town. It was a mile or so up from Godby, the high school from which David graduated. Along with Sector 4 we would stay the night at Creative Preschool where we played our music and raided the big kitchen and dug into cans of peaches and ate from barrels of Animal Crackers meant for the children. We used their finger-paints and paper to make pictures on and finally raided the First Aid kits for fun with the smelling salts. On one occasion, a Sunday morning after Eric and I had spent the night there, we were driving through the neighborhood for home. A kid who was with a group of kids that were doing their own Road Warrior thing, being a little gang and all, threw some gravel as we were driving by. The gravel smattered against Le Voiture. Eric pulled over and jumped out of the car. "You little fuckwad!" he shouted and ran over to the kid, grabbed him by the arm and yanked him towards the car, the kid already screaming and crying, his tough guy façade that he'd put on for the other kids shot to shit. Eric dragged him right up to the car, flung open the back door, and said, "Get in!"

This about scared me to death, and I was glad that Eric let go of the kid's arm. The kid fell on his ass then got up and ran off as fast as he could.

Eric was sincerely pissed off over this little incident, a thing I simply could not understand. Had the kid gotten into the car with us, what then? The situation brought to mind those awful movies they played in elementary school, movies designed to teach us kids ethics, how to distinguish good behaviors from bad and recognize the kinds of situations requiring one to act. One movie projected onto the screen at the head of the classroom showed guys at the beach and there was this girl in a red bikini, and the girl in the bikini was drinking a beer. The movie wanted us to think that drinking a beer made a person want to drink more beer, that the more beer you drank, the more likely you were to do something stupid. Within a minute the girl in the bikini is on her knees in the sand acting like a dog and barking to get more beer. One guy pours beer into her face and she laps at it, trying to get as much as she can. That's how bad she wanted it. The guys are getting drunk too and laughing. Finally, one guy gets in a jeep. He spins donuts in the sand, and then we see through his eyes, the world all blurry—it's what happens when you're drunk. With him, as him, we run over the girl in the red bikini. In another movie it was night out. A bunch of high school guys were in a parked car with a girl. The story leading up to this moment was normal enough—guy picks girl up from her house, tells dad he'll get her home by ten—but then the guys in the back seat with the girl start getting fresh, pawing her and kissing her as she tells them no, don't do that. She looks to the guy in the front seat, her friend that she is out on the date with, for help. What will he do? Oh, what will he do? Will he stop his guy friends from doing what they are doing, thereby alienating himself from the group, or will he sabotage their plan and save the girl?

Ugh, the poor kid leaves the car and runs away from the action and we see him struggling with his conscience in the moonlight as his female friend screams and fights inside of the car. He has the option, we suppose, to pretend like none of this is happening.

What did you learn in school today, dear little boy of mine? What did you learn in school today, dear little boy of mine?

During those early days of the band, the Go-Go's came to town. It was September and they played at the civic center with A Flock of Seagulls. Gary went to the show but I hadn't money for such stuff—it was probably ten to fifteen bucks—but we all met up afterwards outside the Hilton on Monroe Street where the Go-Go's tour bus was parked. We hung around and after a bit Jane Wiedlin, the guitarist and backup vocalist for the Go-Go's, appeared on the sidewalk. Eric and Gary started talking to her. Meanwhile I boarded the bus they'd been touring around in. It's door was open. I just went down the aisle and made myself comfortable in one of the seats. A minute later Kathy, the bass player for the Go-Go's and also the cutest member of the band, came in. It was ten days after my sixteenth birthday. I had the double mohawks going on. The bassist saw me sitting there gussied up like a Road Warrior, but made no effort to get me off her bus. I wanted to go up and talk to her but simply was too afraid. So we sat in different rows, me looking at the back of her head in the silence.

Clearly I was no Road Warrior. I anyway enjoyed very much acting crazy like one and had done so since even before I met Eric, purposely wiping out on my BMX bike to give people a start or make them laugh, walking barefoot over broken glass, jumping out of tall trees and off roofs of houses being built, sticking my foot into a fire and watching it burn and so on and so forth. One day, after getting off work at my part-time job working for the surgeon who also raised beef cows, I staggered out onto Lamberton Road, acting drunk, acting like a zombie, acting like I'd been hit by a car and was dead on the ground, just doing this and that as I waited for Eric to pick me up so we could work on our material. Some 30 minutes into my wait, a Leon County sheriff approached in his cruiser. I was sitting in the middle of the road, legs in front of me, relaxing and probably hoping that when Eric showed up he would see me like this and think, *Yeahp, there's John again, being all crazy, same old.*

The sheriff parked in the cemetery shoulder and got out of his car and said, "Get up and come over here," so I did that, but he put me in handcuffs anyway, saying eight calls had come in about some suspicious character creating disturbances over here. I was like, "Really?" and we got to talking. Turned out he had some American Indian in him, a detail I learned because of the mohawk on my head. The sheriff shared wisdoms then all about the Indians back in the old days. This led me to reveal how my boss was in the KKK. I expected the sheriff to react negatively, but instead he sort of lit up a little and said sure, that some of the sheriffs were in the KKK. We talked about this a bit and he said he could not join the KKK because he had too much American Indian blood, a fact that seemed to sadden him. It was all very strange and he was a fatherly kind of guy with very tanned skin and sensitive eyes. In the midst of this strange discussion, the revving sound of Le Voiture reached us. We looked in the direction of the sound and the little white car appeared at the top of the hill on the other side of the gully. The car dipped into the slope with gaining speed and the sheriff was very interested by this development. He perked up and readied himself for a confrontation, Eric unaware that we were watching him until after he'd bottomed out and was halfway up the hill headed our way. When he saw us, he took his foot off the gas and the car slowed quickly. He pulled over and got out and corroborated the explanation I'd given the sheriff when I first got apprehended, that I was waiting for someone to pick me up to take me to band practice. I was just a kid in a band who worked for the doctor, whom the sheriffs knew of. There was no reason to make a big fuss out of this, so the cop took off my cuffs and let us go, saying to me that it would be in my interest not act so crazy in the future.

That was us.

Of course, I also thought of creeping silently down the hall while my parents slept, entering their room and slamming them over their heads with the hammer we had in the garage.

"Just walk away and the horror will be over," Lord Humungus told the goody two-shoes people barracked behind walls of tin, but the people did not walk away.

And the taut hair preventing me from becoming a terror held firm.

Of other fun times we had during the time we liked acting like Road Warriors, we would stop for pinball and video games at the arcades, which brings me back to those pesky jocks that messed with me sometimes back when I went to Asshole High. They were the kids from middle school who followed me into high school. Some of the animosity they directed my way may have been class-based—they seemed upper-middle while I was only middle, and a weird middle at that—but ever since our band appeared in the paper, on the front page of the entertainments section, no less, same paper thrown by the paper boy onto the driveways of their homes each morning, the jocks were more bristly than usual. The jocks, now, had a defined target.

7.

Our Battle Against the Jocks

FOLLOWING MY JOCK INCIDENT in Waverly Hills, I carried one of my father's golf irons with me wherever I went. Should the jocks try it again, my plan was to mow them down as would the Grim Reaper with his scythe, except instead of harvesting jock souls, I would leave them roadside to rot and fill with maggots. My preference was to never see those guys again, but since classes at SOAR ended earlier than the other schools to facilitate transportation, SOAR being so much smaller than the other schools, first I would take a bus to Leon High, where I transferred onto the bus that took me home. I usually had ten to fifteen minutes before Leon High's last bell rang. One afternoon, I ran like a Road Warrior around the school building several times, very fast with my golf club, and whooped out a few war calls along the way. I had the two spiked mohawks that stuck out like Mercury wings and merged in back, and on my leather jacket was a large 666 symbol. The jocks had seen me from the windows of their classrooms that hadn't yet let out, and also from down in the football field. By the time the bell rang, I was on my bus, slumped in a seat, ready to be carted back to Waverly Hills.

Eight or nine jocks gathered outside the bus. They saw my face—I was easy to spot—behind a window and started banging on the bus with their fists, shouting for me to de-board. Rick Skelter, one of the main jocks, highly revered by the other jocks—maybe he was the richest and most se-cure, I have no idea—started slamming his chest with his fist then pointing at me, shouting, "You and me, come on, let's go!" By the looks of things, Skelter had heard tell of his friends jumping me, and there had probably been talk amongst the jocks about maybe this guy John was a fighter after all, not the weird-ass loser we've always known him to be. John did seem to get the best punches in, after all, get-ting Bruck Smith into that headlock and everything. Wasn't it Bruck who'd walked away with the bloody face after John released him from the headlock?

I looked them over cooly. A jock jumped up and tried hitting me through the pulled-down windowpane. I leaned back, his fist missed. Another jock made slight contact, ruf-fling one of my mohawks. The buses were cued up in an alleyway cutting through the campus. They would move forward a little, then stop, then move forward again until released onto Miccosukee Road, free now to deliver their blobs of matriculant humanity back to the burbs. The jocks saw that there wasn't much they could do save invading the bus, but the driver, Chester, who'd been my driver throughout middle school, even elementary, would not have let them board. The jocks decided to let it go, but as the bus moved forward a step, a kid from my neighborhood, Mark Butler who lived on Lasswade Drive in the stretch of street leveling down against the lake, came along the aisle with a squirt bottle of cleaning solvent. I may have looked calm, considering what had occurred, but my heart beat wonky. My skull felt fat. In this hyped-up state I lumped Mark Butler in with the jocks. Mark Butler had a smirk on his face. I thought he was going to squirt me with the solvent so I jumped up and smashed the plastic bottle between my hands. The top popped off under pressure, and the stuff inside the bottle shot up like a fountain, right into Mark Butler's face. Mark Butler screamed. I was sick of this shit. I grabbed my 7-iron and walked the aisle, Chester eyeing me with a subtle yet complex expression of gratitude—*Thank you for taking it upon yourself to leave my bus.*

With my golf club I walked for home, some four miles if you walked straight, but I always took a different, longer route, going by the malls then walking through the Stoner Woods. I was between malls, the Northwood and Tallahassee, when Eric happened to be driving by in Le Voiture. He pulled over and I got in with him and he said of me that I stood out like a sore thumb. It was the first time I had heard the expression. A sore thumb? What was that? Sounded good to me.

I carried the club to and from school until Janet, who bussed us SOAR kids from SOAR to Leon High, wrote a referral on me, suspending me for eleven days. Janet's reason: "He poked my foot with his golf club and said I was going to Hell," which I had, in fact, done. I had put the handle part of the club on Janet's foot. "You're going to hell, woman!" I said like Jerry Falwell or somebody funny like that. Janet didn't think it was funny. I was off the bus for eleven days.

Gary too had issues with high school jocks, but before I get into them, I should tell you how Gary, a guy who in tenth grade had the great looks and physique to become a jock himself—he was blond with a small nose, of decent physical stature, had a great sense of humor and there was nothing ethnic going on in his features—became entangled with jocks. While attending Leon High, before his transfer to SOAR, Gary was friends with a guy named Clyde. This Clyde was pretty much full-in jock, but Clyde dabbled in bohemianism, and this contributed to Clyde's popularity not only with the jocks, but those who straddled the identity fence.

Unlike Gary, Clyde drank. Since Gary's mom mostly slept with her boyfriend across town, Gary often was alone in the house with his younger sister. Knowing this, Clyde, whose mom never would've allowed underage drinking in her home, convinced Gary to let him store a bunch of beer in his refrigerator. That evening, a Friday, all these people started knocking on Gary's door, and coming in to drink the beer. All these guys and girls. Turned into a party. Gary had had no idea that something like this was going to happen. At one point Gary went into his bedroom and a guy and girl were in his bed making out. The guy said, "Hey dude, you don't mind, do you?"

Do you mind? Kissing in my bed? Gary did mind, but felt restrained from saying it. A panic was building. The emotion was: *I don't want to be a fool by telling them all to get the hell out, but holy crap, I'm hosting a party, this might boost my profile at Leon.* At the party Gary is playing records, Adam and the Ants and the Kinks, people are drinking beer, more girls are coming in, and more guys, these jocks. Eventually the intoxicated kids left and Gary was looked upon somewhat as a hero by the jocks.

This was before Gary was in Hated Youth. Though Gary had the looks to be an in-kid in the jock clique, he hadn't the clout. Gary did not live out in the upper-crust section of Waverly Hills or Killearn. Gary lived in an apartment off John Knox Road close to the Tallahassee mall, and had only one parent, his mom. Gary's dad, an ex-encyclopedia salesman who now sold cars, lived in Augusta, Georgia.

Fast forward to the time Gary is in Hated Youth. The jocks have read the Christopher Farrell article about this massive change in teenage culture going on in their own hometown, and taking place behind their backs. They had seen the photo of Gary and I standing together, two losers, on the front page of the entertainments section of the *Tallahassee Democrat.* These kids had cut their hair, big fucking deal, did that make them celebrities? "Punk," they were calling themselves. Let's fuck up their deal, they said, and said, But wait, didn't Gary host that party that time where we all got trashed and had a great time? Yeah, they said, and said, We can't let them steal Gary from us. We gotta get Gary back! The jocks started casing Gary's place, waiting for the ones with crazy haircuts to show.

It was raining. I was in David's Honda with David. His driver's window had been previously busted out, so David was using a sheet of plastic along with a garbage bag to seal away the rain. When we parked at Gary's apartment complex, this kid clutching a knife, one of Clyde's pals who was also the wrestling champion at Leon High, appeared in the headlights, shirtless in knee-length shorts. The wrestling champion came our way slowly through the rain. He came up to the car and started stabbing through the plastic where the broken window had been. In the process he shattered David's rearview mirror. Right then Eric pulled into the parking lot in Le Voiture. There was some shouting and a brief altercation, after which the guy took off, presumably for backup.

Gary too had been outside, and had seen the whole thing. We went into Gary's place and Gary said, "I'm sick of this shit, I'm quitting the band!" Eric grabbed a broom and slammed it over Gary's back and the broom broke in half. Eric picked up the stick that had broken off and backed Gary up against the wall with it. He jammed the sharp tip into Gary's stomach. "You're not quitting!" Eric shouted. "We've worked too hard on our shit. Don't be like that fucker who bailed out on us in the middle of the night. You're better than that!"

Gary felt, through his shirt, the sharp wood tip pressing into his belly. He made the decision, not right then, but with some heated persuading on Eric's part, not to quit. Gary had been crying even, but Eric made Gary see reason, see the bigger plan. As things progressed, Gary was grateful he didn't quit. Gary knew he chose the right path, just he couldn't be hobnobbing with jocks anymore. Gary made a clean break from the jocks. Gary said goodbye to the jocks.

The jocks did not say goodbye to Gary. The jocks still wanted Gary back. They wanted to use Gary's refrigerator. They wanted to chill out at Gary's apartment and make out with girls in Gary's bed, maybe even fuck Gary's cute sister. A weird war was going on between Hated Youth and the jocks from Leon High.

Once my suspension from Janet's school bus was over, and I was back on my regular transportation schedule, I once again was in radar range of the jocks. Not wanting to incite them, I stayed mellow, just went about my business as I transferred buses. This included, sometimes, walking up towards Freak Hill where the snowcone truck was parked.

One day after getting my snowcone I was walking back down towards the buses. One of the jocks, who had also stood in line and paid for a snowcone, came down behind me. He said, "You fucking faggot," but I ignored him, just kept on walking without changing my pace, which pissed him off because he took his blueberry snowcone and squashed it into my back, thinking maybe it would mess up my long-sleeved white shirt that had random paint strokes all over it. In reality, the "stain" could only add to the overall "punk" look.

But I turned, and as I turned the jock's snowcone dropped to the sunny sidewalk. There he was, his face completely devoid of joy. He'd been so disgusted, so assaulted by the fact that I was setting my own dress code—and also he probably was miffed that both of us could walk along with snowcones at the same time, like *Look, there go two guys with snowcones*—that he sacrificed this little treat he'd been looking forward to slurping on. Strangely enough, or maybe this isn't strange at all, he in later years—and this was true of some of the other jocks too—would fall in line with the "punk rock movement," piercing his ears all "faggoty" and playing in bands, the full works.

My assumption about this jock and the jocks this jock ran with was their dads threw balls to them in their front yards, took them fishing, hunting, bought them rich boy clothes, gave them plenty of money and spoke soberly of their futures. Come weekends they went to church together and all was harmonious and unified in this world where everybody wanted the best for each other so long as they followed the rules. Had I been wiser, less concerned with my place in relation to them, I may have seen something more akin to catastrophe building, a community where the consequences of self-expression were extreme and could lead to violence and ruin.

Even in my own household, which on the surface would have appeared somewhat of an "intellectual" nature that was open to art and free expression, there were penalties for developing opinions or controlling your appearance. When my mother came home from work one day and saw me in the kitchen with a hair-nail jutting from my widow's peak like a horn, completely bald otherwise, she said, "Oh, how sick!" and brought her hand to her mouth in a gesture of shock and repulsion. At this point she was several years divorced from my father. How much harder it must have been for the jocks who had more than just the one parent to contend with.

I did know, of course, that jocks were people too. I just did not have the patience for them anymore, and also they gave me something reasonably worthwhile to hate. In their shadows I saw cops and coaches, duck hunters and the slave drivers of the old South—in short, the people who ran shit.

Another time, while Hated Youth was at Putt Putt Golf and Arcade, I was playing Space Invaders, enjoying my game, having fun shooting the purple, blue, and green aliens when this massive jock came up behind me. He pushed his beefy chest against my back and I turned. Standing before me was my old chum, Jake Hitterman.

Jake lived in the countryside north of town. I'd known him since second grade. In middle school I'd even spent the night at his place a few times. On the paneling that made up Jake's living room wall were framed photos of his older brothers wearing shoulder pads and helmets, doing the quarterback kneel while pressing footballs to the turf. Jake's older brothers were all at the University of Georgia, and played football for the Bulldogs.

Jake showed me around the nearby farms where we weren't supposed to go, and where we picked red bell peppers off the plant and bit into them fresh that way. Jake showed me how potatoes would appear when you dug your fingers into the earthen rows. We scooped some up and threw them at bird houses on poles. The birds who lived in the houses, Jake said, ate thousands of mosquitoes every night.

One morning while Jake's mom grilled pancakes in the kitchen Jake told me about Hairpin Wars, how you'd load a rubber band up with a hairpin. You'd pull the band back, the band stretched between your thumb and index finger, and let go. That's what we played, our hairpins whistling as they torpedoed through the air. Whenever one hit one of us, it stung and left a red dot on our flesh. Jake and I played it in Jake's living room, dodging for cover from one piece of furniture to another, slinging hairpins at each other while diving, laughing, doing the barrel roll. When hit, we'd cry out and pretend to die.

Now here Jake was looking nothing remotely like the fun boy I'd played games with all those years ago, the boy whose house I spent the night in and had played Hairpin Wars with. This new Jake was thick-necked and burly and steely and stony and sturdy as a chunk of metal. He looked so mean and angry, like he wanted to spit, like he wanted to crush my skull between his two hands. "I'll beat your fucking ass, faggot," he said, and inched a little closer.

Jake, now, was in the process of following after his football brothers. At 6'2" Jake played linebacker for Lincoln High and could bench press over 400 pounds. The last time I had spoken to Jake was after I'd returned from Mexico in the sixth grade. One day Jake's family was featured in an article that appeared in the *Tallahassee Democrat*. The article said watch out for people who come to your house and say they will tar your driveway. The article said that the Hittermans were scammed, that after they paid the money to have their driveway paved, the people who paved it disappeared. A few days later, when it was a little bit hotter, their driveway melted and ended up in the street. When I saw the article, I felt as though Jake had hit it big, he was in the news, how crazy and funny was that? I called Jake. I said, "Jake, I'm back from Mexico, I saw that article in the paper." Jake said this and Jake said that and Jake wasn't all that enthusiastic about me having returned from Mexico. I thought maybe we could get back together and play Hairpin War like we used to, but in the course of our conversation I started laughing because the whole thing about their driveway melting and seeping down into the street was so funny. I laughed and laughed and I don't think Jake liked that I laughed. It probably had seemed like I was laughing *at* Jake and his family instead of *with* Jake or about what happened to Jake's driveway. Perhaps Jake had even held a grudge about the laughing that I did about his melted driveway.

Now here Jake was once more, looking into my eyes, crowding me with his pectoral muscles. Eric and David, catching on to the fact that some guy was harassing me, left their video games and rushed over. "What the fuck is this?" Eric said, his confidence through the roof. Jake backed away. When we left the arcade there was a brief car chase around the parking lot, Hitterman with his jock pals chasing us at first then us chasing them. Nothing came of it but later Gary heard tell through Clyde, his connection into the jock world, that Hitterman, known amongst the jocks as the Hit Man, had vowed to destroy Hated Youth. Good luck, old friend!

8.

First Shows, Gary Gets Some, and a Hitler Mustache

HATED YOUTH PLAYED OUTSIDE GAYFERS inside the Tallahassee mall by the fountain during Jerry Lewis's Labor Day Telethon, 1982. Our discordant wall of distortion reverberated through all passages of the shoppers' paradise, against plate glass, in coatracks, across marble and through leaves of indoor plants. Whatever people were doing at the time we broke into song, they stopped it. *What's that noise? Oh shit, it's a band!*

Our first tune that afternoon was "Hardcore Rules," after which we played "Abortion Clinic" and then "Slam Till I Puke." Our 17-song list included "Hey Hey Hey" and "Gestapo High" and "Bacteria On My Dick" and "Je Ne Sais Pas" and "Anarchy" and "I Wanna Kill Them."

Our eleventh number was a speeded-up cover of the Dead Kennedys corker, "Nazi Punks, Fuck Off!" Halfway through it, the cops arrived. They motioned for us to stop playing. We ignored them. A cop grabbed the neck of my guitar. I yanked it away and played on. Again he grabbed it. Somebody pulled the plug right then. Our sound was over, but a photographer from the paper was there. He got a good one of the cop clutching my guitar neck while I smirked into his face, the two of us eye to eye. The photog shot David behind the drums. This was the shot Bob Suren of Burrito Records, 24 years later, would choose to use for the cover of our side of the album he was producing: a Hated Youth/Roach Motel split LP, a 12-inch pressed from Hated Youth songs on a cassette tape.

Hated Youth next played Emmanuel's, a dive bar off Jackson Bluff Road in a part of town considered not good. For two dollars (October 9, 1982) you got to see Hated Youth *and* the Vinyl Punks (their first show) whose music lined up with what showgoers did back then for dancing, how they jumped up and down, often while wiggling their shoulders, jerking, sometimes even snapping fingers. The *pogo*, that dance was called, and the narrow club was just packed wall-to-wall with pogoing pogoers.

Now Lucia had a mentor, a very close friend from childhood who came to Emmanuel's to witness her little sister's initiation into what was sure to become her destiny: a life of poetry and musical performance art that would lead to fame and scandal. But who was this Gary guy? He was boisterous yet shy. He seemed cool. After Hated Youth played, she bumped into him to say what a great singer he was. "You have potential."

She was Jeanette, and soon Gary was in Jeanette's car with Jeanette and Jeanette was telling Gary stories about all these great punk bands she saw in Atlanta, a place she had lived. Jeanette played a song for Gary on her cassette player, saying it was written about her by one of her ex-boyfriends who was in a band. The song was called "Cinderella A Go Go," and was poppy, quirky in the way of the Speedies when they sing, "Let me take your photo!"

Gary was excited but also felt intimidated. This woman who was 20 or 21 was flirting with him while he was only 16. She seemed ancient but was attractive and overloaded with style and she knew about things Gary was interested in. A few days later Gary gets out of class at SOAR, and what's this? Why, it's Jeanette walking down the hall smoking a cigarette. A teacher says, "Hey, you gotta put that out," and Jeanette licks it. She tells Gary she wants to hang out. Gary gives her his phone number. They spend some time on the phone later and the next day Gary skips school and Jeanette comes over while his mom is at her job working for the state. Gary is barely able to talk due to how nervous he is, but they end up in his bedroom. Afterwards, she says, "You were a virgin, weren't you?"

And the day rolled along. At one point Jeanette went into the bathroom. She came out with the word BITCH written in eyeliner across her biceps. Upon returning from work a few hours later, Gary's mom, who had grown up in Georgia and Texas and spoke with a very pronounced southern accent, saw this woman in her house with her son. She said, "Hi," and they exchanged awkward pleasantries. Then Jeanette was gone. Gary's mom went into the bathroom. "Gary," she said, poking her head out, "have you been using my eyeliner?"

A week later, Gary is at SOAR. One of his classmates, Violet Spoon, is flipping through a photo album she brought to school, showing Gary pictures of her relatives, of family gatherings and fun things she did, and pictures of her dad who rode a Harley Davidson. In one picture of her dad, Gary saw Lucia's soul sister standing there and Penny's dad had his arm wrapped around her. "Who's that?" Gary said. "Oh, that's Jeanette, my dad's girlfriend." Gary felt freaked out. This Jeanette was from another planet. Gary had not even known Jeanette was Lucia's close friend from childhood.

That same night at Emmanuel's, the night Gary met Jeanette, after the show, while we packed away our instruments in front of the venue, which was right next to a pool hall, Donny C of the Slut Boys drove through the parking lot in what I will always remember as a black Barracuda with two long-haired college girls in the car with him. "You know I'm gonna beat your ass, Eric!" he said out the window, and then floored it so that the wheels screeched. David was holding a drum. I had my guitar with me. Eric and Lucia were loading our amps into the van. When Donny said what he said, we all turned our heads at the same time. I felt like I was in the movie *Grease* when John Travolta's nemesis, the hoodlum in the hotrod, floors it and flames shoot out the exhaust pipes.

Later that month, on Halloween, Hated Youth and Vinyl Punks played again at Emmanuel's. This time Sector 4 and two other local bands were with us: Generix and the Beloved Children. It was at this show that Gary met yet another hot chick, this one 19 to Gary's 16, which was better than the last time in terms of age difference. This new one was Trudy, and Trudy too had spent time in Atlanta. She loved the band X and was into Psychedelic Furs and knew a lot about music and quickly became Gary's steady girl-friend. Having a girlfriend took time, Gary soon found out, and lots of energy. With a girlfriend, Gary felt himself becoming isolated from the music scene.

Our last show of '82 was in December in Gainesville at the Florida Slamfest, a punk rock bonanza featuring 10 bands. We were not on the bill, but our manager—yes, we had a manager—thought we could finagle ourselves in if we arrived on scene with all our equipment, ready to play. It was worth a shot, so we hopped the divide between our two cities, arriving early at a place in the downtown area called Star Garage, a warehouse type place that had once been an actual garage. Now it was empty of tools and compressors and hydraulic lifts. It was a rentable open space of high walls and corrugated steel. We went inside. A four-foot-tall stage had been built with scrap wood, and some guys were in the process of setting up the massive PA system. There was even a van parked there and somebody was squatting beside it on the concrete, cooking some kind of meat on a Sterno stove.

Our manager asked around about who to talk to and was directed to Bob Fetz, the singer from Roach Motel who had never heard of Hated Youth. Nobody outside of Talla-hassee had. Fetz hesitated in that there were already so many bands scheduled to play. Our manager, who was a lawyer, didn't give up. He said, "Why don't you guys come and play in Tallahassee next weekend at Smitty's?" Fetz thought that was a grand idea, so they shook hands on it. People started arriving—the headcount would reach about 350—and at 9:00 Solid Waste from Gainesville opened the festival with a fast set under a banner that read ETSAW DILOS because they hung it up backwards and didn't have time to switch it back so that it read properly. From the start there were troubles with sound, being the garage was prone to echoes. Hated Youth played next, releasing for the first time to ears outside of their Tallahassee purlieus the sounds of "Hardcore Rules."

Other Gainesville bands rocking the fest were Terminal Fun, Slime (who did a rendition of "Sweet Home Alabama") and, of course, Roach Motel, the headliners. From Tampa came Burning Dogs, Twisted Logic, Rat Cafeteria and Voodoo Idols. The Sluts from New Orleans, brand new album in hand, went wild and crazy on stage, the singer, Dee Slut, jumping and kicking and diving and rolling in glass. In a review of the show published in *Destroy Magazine*, Bob Fetz described the Sluts singer as a bigtime beer drinker and advised that you hide your beer if you get the chance to see the band play. Fetz lauded Burning Dogs for playing a 20-minute rework of "I'm cramped" by the Cramps but censured Twisted Logic for doing too many covers by the Ramones and Sex Pistols. Fetz described Rat Cafeteria as playing "Oi type tunes" with funny titles like "I hate SLUTS" and "Kill the Mentally Ill." As the bands played, people threw beer cans and kicked around skank-style while holding half-filled bottles of beer that splashed as they swung their arms. People slammed into each other, not caring, and everybody seemed to be having a great time.

Some guys had mohawks and the girls too looked great in their colors, unconventional makeup styles and ripped clothes. Other than on ourselves, we'd only seen styles like this in pictures of the UK scene, and in movies like *Road Warrior*. Also there was, of course, that 1981 *Donahue* episode where Phil Donahue's guests are a bunch of punks and their parents. One of the guys on the show had a purple mohawk while sporting a Hitler mustache.

9.

Music at SOAR and Bleeding

OF MY FIRST GUITAR TEACHER AT SOAR, a groovy wavy-haired flip-flop-wearing woman out of the hippie era, Lucia said they'd been naked in a tent during an overnight on the beach at Port Saint Joe. Lucia intimated that maybe there was more to it than that, so I pictured them looking at each other's vaginas in an *Our Bodies, Ourselves* kind of way. I had never seen an opened one save in the dirty magazines I found in the woods, and also, of course, in the book *Our Bodies, Ourselves*, which my mother and every other progressive-minded woman had shelved on her bookcase alongside Simone de Beauvoir and Kate Millet.

Nor did I know what a period was. I had heard people speaking of women "going on the rag" and how that made them bitchy. My boss, the guy I did farm work for on the weekends—he was a throat surgeon too, a man who eventually would go into the liposuction and breast implant business—said even my mom went on the rag. He said this was why we could never have a woman for president, because when women go on the rag they get emotional. If a woman was president, chances were while she was on the rag she would press "the red button" and send nuclear missiles to Russia. Sounded wild and crazy. In truth I knew nothing of the whys and wherefores of menstruation, a word I likely never had heard, either, at that time. What I knew was blood came once a month, and I'd heard people saying maybe all my life that pussy smelled like fish. Maybe I had heard that vaginas farted, too, for how else could I have written that song whose refrain went "Vagina blood fart"? This was one of the first songs I wrote, no music in it, just a pounding on the school desk, two *boom*s with closed fists followed by a slapping down of the flats of the palms. Its beat matched the beat in "We Will Rock You" by Queen.

I recorded the song with Cranford Knight, another SOAR punk, on a cassette tape recorder that we left in the music room. Our amazing workhorse of a principal, the woman who folks said founded SOAR, came around later and grabbed the tape recorder, along with the tape that was in it, and took it with her to a school board meeting on the other side of town. Proudly she entered the room with her unshaved legs on full display. With her were carefully prepared notes and documents, but while doing a sound check, she pressed play on the tape recorder. My song was aired to the superintendent and principals and teachers and all those there to discuss school matters: "Vagina blood fart, vagina blood fart, vagina blood fart, blood fart, blood fart." If you listened on you'd see how the song did not veer as it played out—nothing experimental or nuanced. If you wanted, though, you could imagine a gazillian vaginas farting blood and guts and brains and sinew, a collective blast of human life spilling into the marketplace, onto streets and dripping through branches, a hot pink pulsating rain coming down from the trees.

Well, our principal pressed stop as soon as she understood what was happening. She ignored the stares and rewound the tape and was ready now to record the meeting. The next day, in her office, she was sure to rag me out about it, though she did it with a sense of humor, and she might, even, for the hell of it, have given me a payback.

Cranford Knight, my co-conspirator in vaginabloodfartism, was a cool guy with frizzy blond hair that sort of piled up around his head like a sandy beach ball, a Hated Youth fan who wore to school a jeans jacket vest with the word KILL on the back of it, the letters large and done with black acrylic paint. Cranford drove to and from school in a fiberglass Bradley GT, a springer of a car that he sprung me through Killearn Estates in at topnotch speeds, always trying to run squirrels over, a little game he played in the burbs while stoned—*Let's Kill the Squirrel!* —and maybe drunk sometimes too. Eventually the Bradley GT caught fire during one of Cranford's fast drives and melted on the side of the road, leaving the engine visible inside of a burnt bowl of plastic.

Cranford had been out of control, but since he'd been raised Christian, his mom was into tough love. She hired a hardcore churchy institution type place for teens to kidnap her son and reeducate him at one of their brainwashing facilities. Cranford disappeared for a while. He returned months later healed of sinful associations with punk rock music and druggy behavior. As time went on, Cranford eased back into the punk rock lifestyle, becoming, this time, the type of skinhead to admire Hitler. The Nazi thing Cranford would swear off, like most skinheads would as they grew older, becoming more knowledgeable of the world, but not until after he'd had swastikas inked into his flesh and had spent time in jail over his political entanglements. At heart Cranford was a good dude. He would have preferred singing all about farting vaginas than Blacks and Jews any day of the week. One might even call Cranford a sweet Teddy bear type of guy, and not be far off the mark. Years later, in 1988, when the movie *Child's Play* was released, Cranford identified with the little doll named Chucky who ran around stabbing people with a voodoo knife. He thought it was really funny and scary.

Our next music teacher wore white robes and sandals and looked like Jesus, and our teacher after that was Bill who, compared to our previous teachers, was a square. Bill wore his shirts buttoned up to the neck. He tucked his shirts into his jeans that were cinched tight with a flawless leather belt. Bill's teaching style was the same as his dress style. He liked us all to sit still with our guitars and play shit together, at his guidance, a properly pressed and sounded note here, another properly pressed and sounded note there, all on the G scale.

This thing about learning good form was not to our liking. We budding guitar players wanted to wring the necks of our instruments and make noise, maybe even smash the instruments, but no, we had to sit patiently, be calm, *listen* to what our teacher was saying. We felt like robots, and so one of us said, "Domo ome gato, Mr. Roboto," like from the song by Styx. I could tell Bill didn't like that, so I said it too. Bill said, "Please stop saying that, don't say that again, okay?" I said, "Sure, I won't say it again," but right when Bill started continuing his lesson, I peeped it out. Bill said, "Stop that!" I said "Stop what? Saying domo ome gato, Mr. Roboto?" Bill said, "Yes, if you say it again, I'll give you a payback," so I said, "Yessir," which I had already been saying to Bill and could tell Bill didn't like. Bill said, "And don't say that either." I said, "Yessir," and then I said, "Oh, sorry sir, I didn't mean to say yessir." To that Bill said something but I again said "Yessir," so Bill gave me a payback.

A payback at SOAR is what you got when you misbehaved. One of the teachers gave you a broom and you'd sweep the sidewalks for fifteen minutes, or pick up sticks on the grounds, clean windows or do some other useful thing that maintained the premises. I'm sure I got plenty of paybacks but the one I remember isn't the one Bill gave me for saying, "Yessir" and "Domo ome gato, Mr. Roboto." It was the one I got in the cafeteria for teasing a Black pregnant girl pretty far along in her pregnancy, saying to her, "You're gonna have a dog."

Pretty shitty of me, but it wasn't the only thing shitty in me. As a child I once snatched up the neighbor's barking pug dog and ran off with him into the bushes. He was so danged cute, you know? While in the bushes, just the two of us alone together, I kissed him and squeezed him and "called him George," so to speak. I wouldn't let him go even though he clearly wanted to get back home. This went on for five minutes or so. Another time I had jokingly thrown a heavy stick at a squirrel. I was dumbstruck when the stick hit the squirrel, causing it to fall out of the tree. Worse than that was the time I threw a frog as hard as I could against the street. This act, a cruelty emergent from an inside monologue on life and bravery and the meaning of things, did not play out as I had imagined. Instead of immediately dying, the frog's stomach popped out of its mouth, a shining bubble of you-are-guilty impossible to live down and impossible to forget.

Now as a punk rocker with two spiked mohawks set at angles, a short skinny mohawk trucking through the middle like a one-horned caterpillar, I continued in my scoundrelly ways, having fun all the while. One afternoon I followed two boys in my neighborhood with a long chain that had a jumbled chunk of spiked metal attached to the end. I followed the kids who were maybe a year or two younger than me slowly down Ivanhoe, swinging the heavy chain around me as I walked, letting the chunk of metal on the end of the chain hit the street now and then, sparks flying. The faster I walked, the faster the two boys walked. Then I ran at them with a Road Warrior shout that said I was going to wrap them up in the chain and slaughter them nice and good. The kids ducked into a yard. I followed them. One kid looked over his shoulder, terror-stricken, and tripped into the grass. Both boys screamed but managed to escape. I *let* them escape.

My attitude was anybody not punk was a loser. I may have been angry, ashamed even over how things went in the past, how in first and second grades I'd come home distraught, crying sometimes from school, and my mom did nothing to help fix me. I don't recall being comforted by either parents, only told that tomorrow I'd have to go back to that place, me knowing that the horror would resume, that some kid might stab me in the back with a pencil, or I'd be spit on, or little girls with snarly faces would stick gum in my hair, call me Garbage, their name for me, and hit me, their mocking jubilant laughter ringing and jingling like bells. Or maybe I'd get waylaid by a gang of kids, dragged off into the woods and made to act like a dog and eat shit. Stuff like that could build up over time. Stuff like that could pave your way into a life of creative revenge, and why on earth would I go on to write songs for Hated Youth that included killing my mother? I wrote a song like that even before hearing the Suicidal Tendencies classic, "I Saw Your Mommy," whose lyrics tell the story of a guy who comes across one of his friend's mothers dead and bleeding in a gutter and thinks it's great.

Suicidal Tendencies was a band that spoke to me, a band I could relate to. They were fast, innovative, an un-stoppable, inspiring force of nature, but more than anything else they were fun. "I'm not crazy!" the singer shouted in their song, "Institutionalized," and "You're the one who's crazy," which was exactly right. Before I'd heard them for the first time, my mother had driven me to a psychiatrist to see what might be done with her clearly disturbed mo-hawked son who had stolen her silverware and suddenly seemed to be taking initiative in things, fending for himself and developing his own taste. The little sonofabitch had even come home from school one day with a swastika, about the size of a nickel, penned in blue ink into the hem of his white t-shirt. He sat down at the round kitchen table that way and they were already into their dinner when she saw it. "What's that doing on your shirt?" she said, and he said, "What, this?" as though it were nothing serious. "Wash it off, now," she said. "You're not going to sit at this table with that hateful symbol on your shirt." He started to explain something or other but she wasn't having it. He was lifting a fork of peas to his mouth and she reached over and grabbed his shirt and yanked it off him, peas and fork flying. "Relatives of ours were put to death in concentration camps!" she cried, and that's where the discussion ended.

On the drive to the shrink's office, I had my boombox with me and was playing "I believe" by the Buzzcocks, a seven-minute-long song whose refrain went "There is no love in this world anymore," a lyric that may have been more accurate, if you asked me then, had it gone, "There was never any love in this world to begin with." At the end of the song the refrain is repeated eight times in varying degrees of angst. Finally, my mom cried, "Shut it off, shut it off, I can't take this anymore!" so I shut it off. She told me how this punk rock thing was a phase I would grow out of, that one day I would learn to appreciate real music, that I would come to admire the complexity and meaningfulness of jazz, a transformation that never would, actually, happen. Of all the music available for a guy to listen to, jazz with its nerve-crushing horns, paranoid beats and discursive "adventures" in sound—yeah right—would forever remain at the very bottom of the musical trash heap.

The boys I chased with the swinging chain told the story of how crazy John Hodges chased them through the neighborhood like a rabid human. Word got around that I was a crazy nut, an image that suited me fine. Kids in my neighborhood came to think that I was dangerous and part of a gang, which I was. In the background of me was Hated Eric ever ready to step into the cage with beasts, devils, high school jocks and everyday assholes, for my sake. Somewhat crazy in my own right, I was bathed in the protection of my band of punks.

"Most girls don't like fingers in their vaginas," was another weird thing Lucia said. That was Lucia. She said stuff like that out of the blue. One day, when she and Eric and I were leaving my neighborhood in Le Voiture, I pointed out a neighbor of mine, a girl with red hair and orange freckles whose name, back when we were about ten years old, some of us kids liked to shout out loud, crying "Mary Mahorner" in a singsongy way as we tagged along behind her, laughing, it gave us a thrill. After pointing her out, Lucia smiled hugely and said, with great exaggeration, "Oh, do you want to poke her, John?" which caused my face to turn red even though I'd never had any such thoughts. Perhaps the strangest thing I heard Lucia say was that some girl she knew had bled like crazy after her dad took her virginity. She might as well have been telling us what she had for breakfast. This girl she was friends with, she said, had been having sex with her dad since age four.

10.

The Possibilities of Having a Message

ON MARCH 17, 1983, exactly six months after the Sabra and Shatila bloodbath in Beirut, Hated Eric met with writer Jay Murphy for an interview to appear, along with reviews of the Tallahassee music scene, six weeks later in *Spectrum*. Murphy titled the interview, "An Interview with Hated Eric." Here is Murphy's introduction:

Hated Youth is Tallahassee's only hardcore punk band and undoubtedly the most unpopular on the new music scene. . . Hated Youth's intensity, meth freak speed, and usual indifference to their audience has found more public acceptance elsewhere, at Gainesville's slam fest [1982], for example. Despite near ostracism locally, Hated Youth wins respect from other likeminded bands in Florida and are included in a new hardcore compilation album of Florida bands on the Roach Motel's label, Destroy Records. The LP is appropriately entitled 'We Can't

Help It If We're From Florida' and is due to be released this summer.

Musicians, actors, politicians, celebrities—they notoriously complain of being misquoted, of having their own words used against them or used out of context. Not enough has been said of Hated Youth for me to try to hoard in on that self-loving trend, but I don't recall the feeling of being ostracized, or "nearly" ostracized, I guess because I didn't care and because our "aesthetic," if we had one, was contrary to the notion of acceptance. Since doing our first show as the Little Johnnys on the Union Green, a show that happened, incidentally, on the same day as a major hardcore show in California, one where the Dead Kennedys, Minor Threat, MDC and the Descendents performed, along with Bad Religion, Zero Boys and the Detonators, we had done a dozen shows locally. Then there were the out-of-town events. Seems a stretch to call that unpopular. Our shows were never empty. Besides, we were high school kids. When we played, folks busted out slam dancing. "They were fighting like cats and dogs," my mother's friend Jedrek, who'd driven out Bannerman Road one night to see us play at Smitty's, told her. Jedrek only made it through a few songs before he felt forced to leave.

Jedrek, a worker for the State of Florida who had previously fought as a soldier in Korea, had come to see what was up with his longtime friend's son who'd been cutting his hair all kinds of weird ways and withdrawing from everything normal. On this night in March, Roach Motel headlined for Hated Youth and Daughter Damage. When

HY started playing, Jedrek backed away from the pit, drawing his blond date closer while bringing his other hand up to his mouth in shock. What was going on here?! If you weren't careful you'd get socked in the face.

Had Jedrek stuck around he would have seen guys walk about uncomplainingly with bloodied-up faces, and sure, there was always a chance you could get hurt. How I broke my hand then bit through my lip happened this way: Roach Motel took the floor in the yellow light at the end of the rectangle, opening their set with a rumbling bass and feedback creeping in. The combination of sounds opened the gates to the reservoirs of adrenaline. George Tabb, standing with legs wide apart, slid his pick down the fretboard, Bob Fetz jumping forward with a growly "Ahhhhhh!" as though attacking headlong into a thing. The first chord struck. The floor erupted in mayhem, in wild, chaotic, out of control violence.

After four rounds of the central chord progression, Fetz shouted, "I hate the Sunshine State" five times, and then: "Old people everywhere. Rednecks, Cubans and what's worse. Frat boys and new-wave fags who forgot where they left their purse," a song with a message! Fetz was a new and improved Darby Crash in ways—the ache was there and the growl but the words were sharp, no abstractions, you could understand what the singer was saying. If you wanted to take the lyrics at face value, that was up to you, but for me it was more like a story and charade. What they did and what they were doing seared the air around them in a yellow fizzy elongated bubble of astonishing action.

A chorus of another song ran, "Where the hell's your fuckin' green card?" repeated four times and followed by "Wetback" a bunch of times. Before I'd heard that song, I didn't know what a wetback was, nor what a green card was. I asked our manager about it, "What's a wetback?" and Mike, God bless him, explained the thing about the Juarez River, how when Mexicans crossed over into the United States, sometimes their backs got wet.

At one point during Roach Motel's set, when the pit was thick with energy, I hopped up on Smitty's bar top and ran across it and jumped, arms out cruciform. My head and hands bashed against the ceiling. Down I went into the slam dancers whirling below, my face slamming onto the top of David Fats' head. I bit through my bottom lip. Tasted blood. Dropped to the floor and got up and skanked on in the frenzy of elbowing bodies, blood pouring out of my mouth and getting on my clothes and the clothes of others. At the end of this blast of group energy, the pain crept in. My hand was tender and hot. I'd broken it on the ceiling of Smitty's.

In the Jay Murphy interview, Hated Eric says of the show we were scheduled to play the following day (March 18, 1983) at the American Legion Hall in Gainesville: "This Minor Threat gig I feel pretty confident about. We're going in there, Gainesville, our guitarist has a broken thumb in a cast but he's still going to play. We might even take the show."

We'd heard Minor Threat's EP that begins, "What happened to yoooooou, you're not the same." Eric had it. Eric always got ahold of the great music right when it came out. He had connections in California, like with his brother

Clark and other people he knew. Eric visited the Tallahassee record stores often, always adding stuff to his collection. And whenever he visited California to see his brother Clark, he came back with another stack of cool records. He was a collector.

The Minor Threat EP about killed us with enthusiasm, an appreciation for the escalating musicianship and artistry entering the scene. Years later I would trace the techniques Minor Threat used to the Circle Jerks who may have been the truest pioneers of that fun-time skank-through-the-park sound that became so popular. If not the Circle Jerks, who? Certainly not the Bad Brains who were their own forest of wild. Though other bands adopted elements of reggae to be more like the Bad Brains, I don't recall hearing fast riffs that much crossed theirs. Black Flag too seemed self-contained while MDC and 7 Seconds were ratcheting things up a notch with that urgent, searing, skin-you-alive sound that also was catching on and making the rounds. The bands were learning from each other. Minor Threat felt new, but if you listen to them now on the same day as Necros and Negative Approach, to name just two other bands, you'll hear similar chord progressions and vocal inflections, enough to make you wonder, despite the order of their releases, who came first. Was Minor Threat the chicken or the egg? They were featured in the latest issue of *Maximumrocknroll*. Eric held the magazine open for me and pointed at the black-and-white photo of the bald guy gripping the mic and looking hard and angry. "Check out that widow's peak, man. This guy fucking means what he says!"

We drove down there, about 150 miles, and did our sound check inside the large open venue—wood floors, high stage, elaborate sound system and a wall that had been turned into a gallery of framed black and white photos, stacked three high, of fallen World War II heroes. While Minor Threat sound-checked, one of the two Roach Motel guitarists, Jeff Hodapp, was standing beside me. He observed that the songs Minor Threat played to get ready for the night were by the Damned. Who were the Damned? I had never heard of the Damned.

Minor Threat's standoffish singer, once things were set up but before the show started, stood at a payphone outside the American Legion Hall talking, somebody said, to his mother in D.C. With his white smooth head and doughy pale arms he looked ghostly, like an inscrutable and possibly malevolent Pillsbury Doughboy, just without the chef's hat—rare, mythical, larger than life.

Moral Sex played first, then Sector 4, then Hated Youth. As my left arm and thumb were wrapped tight in a plaster cast, my chord-pressing and movements were limited, but I still could use my fingers curling out of the cast's end, which I had filed away here and there to make playing easier. Taking the stage, I got down flat on my back with a pillow behind my head. It was a big show, hundreds of punks and hardcore people slamming out there. Nearing the end of our performance I stood up and played using my cast as a slide up and down the fretboard, making my guitar make weird sounds, treating my guitar with great disrespect. Like my amp, my guitar was substandard, a cheapy that seemed designed for thrashing around. It was durable and there was no great loss in destroying little pieces of it. After a bit of that Eric and I exchanged instruments. I slid my cast up and down along the fat strings of his bass. We were trying, without having planned it, to go out with a bang in the way rock musicians do when going overboard with reverb and smashing things onstage.

For our grand finale I unstrapped myself from Eric's bass. I lifted it over my shoulder and cocked it back like a spear. I sent it flying into the crowd of skinheads and punk girls. They moved back as the speeding bass shot their way, headstock forward, in slo-mo, tuning keys flashing. The bass was about to draw blood, poke eyes out with its haywire whiplash string-ends that hadn't been cut—a nanosecond more is all it needed—but the slack in the cord gave out and the bass stopped short of its target. Eric's bass dropped to the floor like a vampire on the end of a leash, at which point a chunky skinhead in combat boots and flight jacket jumped up and down on it.

Roach Motel played next, followed by Minor Threat who were amazing as expected—tight, fresh, fast, interesting. They looked and sounded super intelligent. The Pillsbury singer guy threw up the mic cord while shouting, leaning back at times and looking like he might topple over. He flung sweat and spat liquids and wiggled his fingers and it was very photogenic and entertaining to watch and hear. I loved how they'd stop in the middle of a song, on a dime, as the saying goes, opening a door to a silence that they then slammed shut, resuming the music without any cue from the drummer. Unbelievable. And the people there knew the lyrics and sang along: "Guilty of being white!" they wailed, their bald heads shiny and bobbing like an army of fishing floats in the wake of a passing jetski. As you might imagine, some did the Hitler salute while screaming it out. I don't recall seeing a single Black face.

Before Minor Threat started their set, Hated Eric had secured a gang-nail plate around my plaster cast. If you don't know what a gang-nail plate is, it's a flat strip of galvanized steel with dozens of razor-like nails poking up, a thing you see laid across the seams of A-frames, what carpenters use to connect boards as they build houses to get money to support families, all that. Eric and I had been drinking from a flask of Canadian Mist. When Minor Threat started up, I went skanking, slamming into folks, cutting up arms, blood flying until folks saw what was what and backed away. At one point I went in the bathroom to see streaks of blood. It was like somebody had dragged fingers over the wall before collapsing onto the floor. Did I, I wondered, have something to do with that? Some guy, I heard later, lost an eye that night skanking in the pit.

Near the end of their set, and possibly this was their last song, Minor Threat fell into something slower that was different from what they'd done so far. Everybody knew the lyrics of this one too. The skins locked arms. They went in circles kicking and singing out in the same tone, one might say, of "For he's a jolly good fellow"—that was the vibe, of bonding at the end of the night, the lyrics droning on about a stone, "I'm not your stepping stone," yes, I had heard it before. Though we'd never had cable at home, now and then I caught snatches of *The Monkees* at houses of kids in my neighborhood. Minor Threat was doing that song that

The Monkees did. The lyrics must be very important and meaningful, I thought.

Our most diehard fan, Cody Brains, talking years later of that same night, said, "Yeah, I went in the bathroom to take a piss and there was this chick, dude, she was on the floor and all these skinheads were holding her down and fucking her. One guy looked at me and said, 'Are you a man?' I had to get out of there, dude." Cody Brains would confess to me, once he learned I'd started writing this book, that he hadn't been at the Minor Threat show, only the Negative Approach show that wouldn't go down for another 15 months. The girl-in-the-bathroom story was either made up or had happened somewhere else that night in the world.

The Jay Murphy interview with Hated Eric came out in *Spectrum* a few weeks later, and in it people saw, for the first time, something resembling a philosophy attached to the name Hated Youth. Hated Eric said:

> When I first moved to Tallahassee I wanted to start a band when I saw the Slut Boys. I thought somebody has to realize what is going on here. Everybody's idea of God was Iggy Pop. When I wanted to get a band together, I wanted to put out a message. I didn't have a message in the beginning, for a long time I didn't realize what Hated Youth was going to do. Basically what Hated Youth is doing, is showing to Tallahassee, to Tallahassee especially because Tallahassee is so Bible Belt, is that kids nowadays, in schools, are working for this future that isn't even there. There's this huge end in the back of their minds, and people will sit back

and say, "I don't want to think about it, but you think about it, you worry about it." But whether you worry about it or not, it's there.

Eric had written a song about the Bible and the bomb after our mutual boss, the farmer surgeon guy I mentioned before, the guy whose ancestors had owned slaves, a fact that much pleased him, said if the world ended due to nuclear bombs it would be God's will. Your "future" wasn't guaranteed. Futureless futures came up often in punk rock. The futurelessness of our futures was a workhorse in lyricism. Even big notable Johnny Rotten had crooned, "No Future," in the Sex Pistols smash hit, "God Save the Queen." To fix the future you'd have to dismantle and recreate the current establishment, which could be done and had been done in the past in various places. Was not the end result, though, of revolutions, give or take, that you ended up where you started? It was a waste of time so fuck the future. Embrace pleasure. Stand up and shout, adding your voice to the stand against war and oppression and every imaginable manner of stupidity. Not to change things, but for the hell of it . . . for fun.

Eric told Murphy, "The Bible programs people, and the people behind it program everyone else in America to think that man has this limit, this height of technology and that there is a limit and that God is going to decide."

Of the Tallahassee punk music scene, Eric told Murphy: "I've been told that Smitty's has the most violent scene anywhere in Florida, but then I heard that when Crucial States and the Abusers were down in Miami they had a real heavy crowd. We're into having kids come out and hear our stuff. I'd rather play for twelve-year-olds rather than anyone else. I like kids more because they can go out there and get hurt and laugh it off. . . We're just doing something to keep ourselves from being totally bored."

Message? Well, people said Ronald Reagan was bad. So was Ronald McDonald. I didn't care. People said Hitler had been horrible, but Hitler was dead, so why care? Because "THOSE WHO DO NOT REMEMBER THE PAST ARE CONDEMNED TO REPEAT IT"? That's the slogan our smooth-talking preacher man, Jim Jones, was fond of. In real life and in the movie starring Powers Boothe that I had watched on our B&W TV one Sunday morning, enraptured when I was about ten years old, Jones kept the phrase displayed on a signboard above his chair in the common area where he preached. It was an interesting yet perplexing slogan because remembering the past could as easily, it seemed to me, compel one to repeat it, either as victim—*Take me into bondage in exchange for a bauble*—or as aggressor—*Get on your knees before my Bible!* No matter how grisly, ass-backwards or cruel the past may have been, somebody somewhere at some point was sure to be like *Hey, thanks for the idea!* Getting to know human beings a little more with each passing year, the reality of the golden rule, in practice, seemed more to be, Do Unto Others As You Would Never Have Them Do Unto You.

But we didn't think that stuff out. We just wrote shit down, or didn't write it but shouted it out on the spot, like Gary did with, "I wanna join the Army Dad!" which he shouted over and over and then shouted, "Kill, till I'm dead, till I'm dead, till I'm dead!" Like many of our songs, it was born by surprise, and though it sounds extremely fast, only a true hardcore aficionado might determine that I was getting an extra note in on each beat with my guitar playing, playing not two quarter notes in typical up/down fashion, but doing quarter notes followed by two sixteenth notes, or down strokes paired with down-and-ups. Due to my shitty equipment, this aspect of my strumming was mostly buried in a wall of sound.

Another of our songs, a favorite of mine to play, was "Kill the Punks." It began with me going crazy on guitar, all sorts of trickly high pitched crushings, a smashed harp, then Gary shouting: "That's just what I wanna do, they don't need us, we don't need you. Now we're gonna kill 'em off, we don't need 'em anyhow." Like a flying knife-wielding superhero Gary broke into the chorus with "Kill a punk!" after which Eric came in, antistrophe, with "Rocker," back and forth they went, "Kill a punk!" from Gary, and then "Rocker!" from Eric. Kill a punk rocker. That's it. Fuck those assholes and the jocks and everybody else in the world. They were all the same. That was the attitude. "Kill the hippies!" and, "I hate jocks!" We fantasized about killing. Perhaps this was the mindset of your average eighties' teenaged loner.

In that same issue of *Spectrum*, penned by an unnamed person, likely Steve Dollar judging by the snap-crackle-pop prose flourishes, wrote, "Hated Youth whip up a loudfast cyclone of agitated noise – burly bruising rhythms and tachycardiac riffing." The writer goes on to say, "Politically, Hated Youth are confused, denouncing Reagan and 'Nazi

Punks' while adopting a stage stance that is nothing if not fascist – but blame that on Hated Eric."

I think we could blame everything on Hated Eric, both good and bad, just for fun. But the contrariness of Hated Youth made sense to me. Whatever you were called, whether a fascist or humanitarian, you still were the same as the other guy, which made all that complaining a lot of hypocrisy. Like that *stepping stone* business. All those people at the Minor Threat show were shouting out that they didn't want to help some barefooted girl get a leg up in life. Seemed miserly and mean. The band and those there to see them had the *lets be good people* vibe going on, and yet they wanted payment for kindnesses. Instead of wanting to be used, they wanted credit, recognition for themselves. At the end of the night, the skinheads ripped the pictures of the war heroes off the wall, the glass frames breaking on the floor.

I'm not your stepping stone, mother fucker!

Jay Murphy, I think it is worth noting, had been a student of my dad the Commie, a kind of disciple, if you will, who followed the line that Capitalism was to blame for the world's ills. Murphy edited a communist rag called *The Red Bass* and adored rebellious music. It came about that Hated Youth played a party at Murphy's house one weekend. I had my mohawks looking good and felt great playing guitar. I was aggressive and rowdy and maybe, as a performer, stealing the show. Though I never had nor never would make any effort to steal any show, and though I had thought we were up there working together, knocking people out with our performance, Hated Eric didn't like to see me getting attention. As our show ended, I peeped something out, some kind of acknowledgement of the love we were getting, the clapping of hands and the cheers. I guess it touched a raw nerve in Eric. Right then, in front of everybody, he told me to shut the fuck up and jumped up and kicked me with both feet. It knocked me down and I took off my guitar and ran outside through the night and found a place to be alone and sulk and think things through, like what happened? Was this a repeat of how things had been years ago when feeling rejected and scorned by my family I would run outside and hide in the bushes and cry my eyes out, feeling sorry for myself? Was this what was to be expected, always and forever, of the people I would meet in my future?

11.

Weed, Quaaludes, Shrooms

MY LIFE IN DRUGS began the day I dragged dregs with Nick and this older guy Robby, a gay stoner boy from the Lakeshore neighborhood west of Meridian Road. While in seventh and eighth grades, I bought bags of redbud from various shady characters I met at the mall, Columbian my favorite, all sorts of ragweed and homegrown skank. It took money. I made some from the racist farmer I worked for, tackling his calves into the hot grass while he punched holes in their ears or elasticated their balls, but also I dipped into my mom's silverware box from time to time, stealing off with forks and knives and spoons that my older stoner connections pawned for me at a jewelry store across from the Northwood Mall, secretly taking their cut, of course, as middlemen before sliding back into the car. I did Quaaludes. I drank wine, beer, whiskey. I grew weed on the roof of our house. The whole thing about growing breasts from smoking the stuff turned out to be a big fat lie. A point came where I stopped checking my chest in the mirror to see if I was turning into a girl.

With Eric I snorted the speckled powder that came out of Black Beauty capsules. The little black balls in there looked like poppy seeds—that's where the good stuff was, Eric said. And I swallowed Yellow Jackets. I did shrooms with David and Eric at somebody's house, I don't know whose, where for five dollars you got a Ziploc sack filled with shrooms already boiled down. We mixed our shroom juice with red Kool-Aid in the kitchen and I took my tall glass of it to the living room where a bunch of people watched a VHS recording of the punk episode of *Donahue*, the show that aired first in 1981. Here Donahue talked with parents as to their punk children, asking, "Aren't we obliged as parents to love our children unconditionally?" to which one mother said she'd rather see her daughter on drugs than with a purple mohawk.

I drank the tall glass of Kool-Aid down. The TV started floating. It floated over the heads of the others there. It floated through the room. This was the beginning of what I'd have to call a night of agony, or bad trip.

After *Donahue* David drove me over to the Unitarian Church off Meridian Road. The church was set back in the woods a little ways and Sector 4 was inside the church practicing. We said goodbye and David drove on and there I stood. Beyond the tall spear-shaped windows elbowy figures jabbed the air. Streaks of color and sound came out and like fingers pushed me into the woods. All these twigs scratched my face and arms. I waded through spider webs and sticker bushes. I crossed Meridian Road into my neighborhood. Walking for my house at two in the morning up Lothian Drive, the planet was like a ball. I walked on it and it turned below me while I stayed in place. Once my house popped up, I walked across the yard to the front door. I put my hand on the knob. I slowly turned it. The sound was so loud. This assault against the silence had the blood pumping through my heart at an enormous rate. Once inside my house the silence expanded and every tiny little noise became huge. My sounds echoed down the hall where my mother, divorced from my father, slept at the end. Sweat ran down my face. I felt like a thief in my own house, which I was. I stepped light. Haltingly. Then I was in my room. On my bed and the room transformed into an overturned barrel that started rotating. I ended up on the ceiling staring down. I didn't know how I stuck to the bed, upside down as I was. To try and stop the craziness I turned off the light, at which point demon-like figures emerged from the digital clock. These demons jumped around the room all fiery and red.

This went on. It kept going on. It went on a lifetime, it seemed, but then was over. I made it to school. I got stoned. After school I hung out with Eric north of town.

I dropped LSD at the outdoors Psychedelic Furs show we drove down to Gainesville for. Our Daughter's Wedding were to open for them, so the excitement was high. Gary and his girlfriend even backed into their parking space so that the people in the field could see Trudy's awesome PFURS license plate. She and Gary had hoped the band might see it, or catch on that somebody had it, and be happy about it or who knew but that Gary and Trudy might get an invite to party? As the Furs played, Paul from Sector 4, described once in the paper as the "incredible shrinking drummer" jumped up on stage and gave a good skank.

Eric especially loved LSD. He and Lucia would do it together and one night, while tripping, Lucia woke up Eric's parents by being loud and rowdy. Eric told me about it years later in detail, saying, "I took my finger like this"—he stiffened his middle finger—"and jammed it against her clitoris," and he demonstrated the gesture in the air.

Shortly afterwards Lucia moved out of the band room at the bottom of the crushed stone driveway. I helped her pack her car with her books and bags of clothes and sundry items such as the collar and leash she'd been attached to while Eric walked her through the Governor's Square Mall as a female slave, soon getting the attention of the security guards, the two of them causing a great big scene. As we loaded her car, Eric on the floating back porch of his parents' house shot at squirrels with a BB gun.

Waking up his parents wasn't the only thing Eric took issue with when it came to Lucia. He could not stand that she smoked cigarettes. Her brand: Gitanes, made in France. Damn things smelled like cat piss. And were bad for you. Eric said stop it but then found her with a new pack. He crumpled them up so she couldn't smoke them. This kind of thing led to arguments. He was controlling, rude to her in public. One time when we were over at the Sector 4 house on Macomb Street where three punk girls out of Rickards High—Amy, Jennifer and Bonny—also lived, Eric had some good weed that he wanted to bust out with everybody. He wanted to roll a joint, but the papers were down in the car. He asked Lucia to get them. When she hesitated, he said, "Go down and get the papers you fucking bitch!" and she did.

That was Eric. Sometimes, not always. If he wasn't being super nice to you, he might be in the opposite mode of spiteful meanness. He could be petty, but isn't this true of everybody, to a degree?

I drove out with Lucia to her new apartment and helped her get set up. One item I'd helped pack into her car was the school desk chair combo we stole from the North Florida Christian School that night they brought over *In Watermelon Sugar* for me to read. Lucia could sit in it now and write poetry. Together we carried it inside her sparse new digs where Lucia lit up a Gitane. She crossed through the living room into the bedroom and, without closing the door behind her took off her shirt. In the wisps of smoke she changed into some new clothes, not minding that I could see her bare back and small breasts when she turned to the side. During this interchange, where our talk was spliced with awkward silences, Lucia said, "You're going to be so cool when you're twenty."

12.

Arrogant Fathers and Wendy's Hamburgers

WHEN THINGS DID NOT GO ERIC'S WAY, Eric wasn't happy, and sometimes expressed his displeasure with anger directed at people he cared about. He wasn't the only one. My mom liked being in control. The cops liked being in control. Our teachers liked being in control. If being in control was a part of life, and if being in control made you successful, why not make an effort to be good at being in control? If you weren't good at being in control, good luck getting what you wanted out of life, or what you thought you wanted because who knew for sure what they really wanted?

"What do *you* want, John?" Eric would say in a icky voice, like when we were riding in the car and he was feeling mean. "What do *you* want?" as if I was below the level of wants, or that's how I took it. In truth I may have wanted what he had: good pussy, though I never would have admitted it, not even to myself. But we were male. We were men. And even Gary one day had said, about some hamburgers we'd picked up from Wendy's, "Smells like pussy," the look on his face the look of a guy in the know. Simply put, there was nothing in the world more impressive, more mysterious, more compelling, than pussy.

Natural then that Eric should write songs about the "botooo," as he called it, sidling by on sidewalks and streets, driving in cars with clothes on, shifting gears, pressing clutches and doing all the awesome things women do throughout their days. "You have beautiful eyes," Eric told the girls running the registers at Wendy's. This made them love him, you saw it in action, how a compliment moved a girl, how a compliment made her step back, maybe lift her fingers to her mouth as she lowered her chin, and smile. These gestures made them look inferior to the image I had of them as impeccable mysteries. To me, "girls" were more intelligent, more knowing of things than guys, more under-standing and also they were cute and grew titties. Why, then, were they so easily manipulated? I didn't like this.

As Lucia wasn't into being controlled, problems arose between her and Eric, and Eric even wrote a song he titled "Clap Trap," about loose women without scruple who spread their disease around by fucking too many guys. Gary had to sing that song, a song he suspected was about Lucia, which maybe it was. Gary didn't like singing it, but this was Hated Youth, after all—there had to be the forward-blast-ing passion and sense you believed what you said. All our songs went that way, no drawing lines. The virtues of hard-core thrash were speed, tightness, no pauses between songs, and appearing to believe what you said. All four were a must.

Then Eric wrote one called "Five Sides" about girls collectively, how girls don't understand what guys want and that's why they get abused, like they deserve it. Gary sang that song too, screamed it like he meant it, this thing about hey, you know what, I wanna fuck you and you act like you're into it but then when I try to fuck you you pretend like you don't wanna fuck me back. That's why you've got a beatdown coming on. In later years Gary hoped lyrics to the song wouldn't surface to point a finger at him, saying *Look what you said!*

To be sure, many of the era's punk and hardcore songs were going to turn corrosive in the ears of later generations and did. What we had taken as homespun fun would be labeled offensive, causing more daring bands to censor themselves. Roach Motel chose to leave their wetback song off a reissue of their album, never mind that it may have been the most anti-deportation song ever recorded. Why? Because it ridiculed the Border Patrol with a special finesse and made people who didn't like Mexicans look supremely stupid and lacking. Also, and sadly, it told the truth. But even our fun-loving coffee-drinking ultra-nerds, the Descendents, at some point, would stop performing "I'm not a Loser," a song voicing the expectation that a girl should fuck you if you get her high on coke, a song that also seemed to ostracize gays. "Homo-sexual," by Angry Samoans, on the other hand, was guaranteed to age well. The Samoans knew how to be funny without crossing the line of satire and ventriloquism into a realm people of the future might feel compelled to call hate speech. As per the Samoans envelope-pusher, "The ballad of Jerry Curlan," where a guy named Jerry is depicted as sucking dog dicks and fucking his mother and eating his dad's asshole and stuff like that, it was so over-the-top that it could not ever be anything other than hilarious.

The Sluts had a song called "Mother's Cunt." That too was funny, but in another of their songs, one about Black people, and one I saw them perform at the '82 Slamfest, the singer droned, "Slow, the way they work."

Other than just a few songs, Gary loved it all, and loved screaming, "Theodore Bundy is sick in the head, all you women better not go to bed." The Bundy one was mine, its refrain: "If I had a gun, if I had a knife, I'd blow his fucking brains out I'd rape his wife!"

Another song Gary loved singing was "Fuck Russia," a song he and I wrote together one day while sitting on a stack of tumbling mats during gym class at the School of Analytical Reasoning, our backs against the cinderblock wall. Grayball, as I liked to call Gary—this to do with a big cyst on his head—had his notebook open and, without any forethought, wrote down the line: "We've got a toilet but we shit on you." Under Grayball's line I wrote, "you're a fucking Commie and we don't need you," after which Grayball wrote, "Russia Russia Russia Russia," and I wrote, "Ronald Reagan's gonna flush'ya." Grayball wrote, "We're the few the proud the strong," and I wrote, "We're the ones who got the bombs." All that, unchanged, became the chorus for our song, "Fuck Russia," you can listen to it right now on YouTube.

Later that day we put the song together in the band room after snorting Black Beauty powder dumped out of hard-shelled capsules—an instant classic! My dad was, you know, known around the world as a Commie. He'd been to Russia. He even had, so he said, a bank account in Moscow. My dad did not believe in gewgaws and music and stupid-ass children. Is that why I wrote the line, "You're a fucking Commie and we don't need you"? My dad had wanted to join the Hitler Youth when he was a kid growing up in Argentina, but his parents, who were Dixiecrats, said no. He still admired Hitler, *Mein Kampf* a book that never strayed too far from his writing desk. He thought the name of our band should be called, not Hated Youth, but the Brownshirts.

Another song of Gary's that to me seemed pure us, and this was put together early in the band, was called "Total Control" and the line I liked so much went, "I don't know why my life's in the dirt, my dad tried to kill me with an Izod shirt, just refused to fit his mold, he tried to teach me, just do what you're told!"

It came from the time Gary visited his dad in Augusta, Georgia. During the visit, Gary's dad started showing off about what a great job he was doing fathering Gary's sister, eighteen months younger than Gary, who lived with their dad in Georgia now while Gary lived with their mom in Florida. Gary's dad was on the couch in the living room while Gary sat in the Lay-Z-Boy. His dad is drinking scotch, saying, "So what do you think, Gary? What do you think of Jarma? Isn't she blossoming? Look at how great her environment is. Be honest, Gary, tell me what you think."

Gary said, "I don't think anything about it."

Gary's dad was like, "Well, what do you think, I mean, look at her? Isn't Jarma doing good? I think she's blossoming."

All this was in the context of Gary's dad having mocked Gary's being the singer of a punk rock band. Gary could not escape the feelings he was having, which were mixed, so didn't say what he knew his dad wanted to hear. Gary did not say, "Oh, Jarma seems like she's doing great," or say, "Jarma's got it good, Dad." He did not say, "This is a great arrangement," or, "I wish I lived with you instead of Mom." No, what Gary said was, "I think Jarma and her friends are a bunch of losers," because Gary had gone out with them and he knew that they were smoking pot and drinking, something Gary did not do.

"Losers?" his dad said. "Losers? Look at you!"

It was like being in the Twisted Sister video where the dad screams at his son: "What're you gonna do with your life?"

Gary's dad is just sitting there. He is drinking his scotch and he can't believe Gary just called his sister and her friends a bunch of losers. He says, "You really think they're losers, Gary?" and Gary says, "That's *riiiight*, Buddy."

Gary's dad jumped off the couch and jumped on top of Gary and the Lay-Z-Boy went through all the clicks, falling straight back so that it was on an even plane with the floor and Gary's dad is just choking Gary, choking his son and spit is coming out of his mouth and he's yelling at Gary.

After that Gary said he wanted to go home. Next day, without even speaking to Gary, Gary's dad drove Gary to the Greyhound bus station. Gary rode the bus home and resumed his life as the singer for Hated Youth.

A week or two later Gary came across a letter his dad wrote to his mother, and in the letter his dad says, "How can you let Gary go around looking like a freak? I was embarrassed by him," all this because of the earring Gary wore in his left ear, two piercings in the same ear. Gary's hair was short. Gary sometimes put safety pins in his shoes, but not for style—it made his shoes last longer, and Gary felt that he could do with a new pair. He wore shirts with no sleeves. Nothing big. That made Gary a freak. But it was just his dad being controlling. In Gary's song about the incident, he screams, "Society's got total control, dad's entrapped and can't let go, in the end he will pay."

Years later Gary's dad paid. He paid by learning that his daughter, twenty-two, overdosed on drugs. The daughter of Gary's dad did not die from the overdose—*thank you Jesus!*—but it was a close call. The shit showed Gary's dad that Gary was not the druggy punk loser he'd thought Gary was. When the overdose happened, Gary was soaring across the Indian Ocean as a respected sailor in the United States Navy.

13.

Hated Eric's Musical Gestation

TWELVE-YEAR-OLD ERIC RODGERS walked into the PX on the base at Moffett Field in Santa Clara County and bought his first record, an LP by the Commodores. The artwork wasn't great. It was a random buy his mom paid for, but when Eric played it on his parents' all-in-one Panasonic stereo system, he felt giddy with an appreciation for how the sounds fit together. The music exercised his sense of taste, and he felt as if he'd bought into something that could gain value over time, the main hit here being, "Brick House." It was about a woman who was "mighty-mighty." This woman had "everything," was "stacked," and went around "letting it all hang out." Eric sang along with it while it spun on the turntable, and also sang it while out in the world— "She's a brick house." It was pretty awesome.

This album by the Commodores, 1977, marked the start of a passion for vinyl that would accrue over the years, sucking up Eric's time and resources—space too—but it was worth it. Collecting music gave Eric a sense of purpose. His mission was to find the gems.

The following year Eric's brother Clark started taking him to shows in San Francisco, a thirty-minute drive from their cul-de-sac off Berryessa Street on the east side of San José. The Dead Kennedys, one of the first bands Eric saw in San Francisco, changed his life. He bought their single, "California Über Alles," and then in 1980 grabbed up their first LP, *Fresh Fruit for Rotting Vegetables*. What a masterpiece. "Holiday in Cambodia" was the shit.

Together Eric and Clark saw Peru Ubu, the Plastics, Tuxedo Moon, and the Germs whose singer had the problem of not keeping the mic up at his face. As Eric was young and new to the stuff, he hadn't quite clicked in with the groove of discord going on. The inchoate moaning aggravated him, but he bought the Germs record produced by Joan Jett. He loved it. Eric and Clark saw the Bad Brains who came onstage with flying V guitars, jumpsuits with sequins all shiny, playing fast. They saw 7 Seconds, impressive as a three piece, the Fall, James White and the Chances (aka the Contortions). They saw a local band in San José called ½ Church. Then there was Eric's brother's band, Thieves Cross. There was Flipper from San Francisco. Throbbing Gristle. Eric saw Random Hold open for Dire Straits.

Most of the vinyl Eric bought was from Rough Trade—only two outlets in the world, San Francisco and London—whose whole inventory was two stacks. The store couldn't've been ten feet across. You walked in, there were two bins that you looked through. The records were expensive. He'd buy a few at a time, but when he had a big chunk of change he'd drop a hundred dollars.

Eric's first money came from doing lawns. Then he got into selling hash and the bankroll fattened. He'd get a kilo, a thousand grams for nine hundred. That was dirt cheap. It was straight from Lebanon, had a Lebanese seal, a big stamp in hot red wax on cheesecloth. Eric sold grams for eight bucks. A thousand grams equaled eight thousand bucks. Eric sold the stuff out of his parents' house. People he didn't know were coming over to score. Cops started casing the place. Eric became more cautious.

Through hash, then, Eric bought the Bang & Olufsen turntable and Bose 901 Series IV speakers, a source of pride. Dropping the stylus into the vinyl groove he knew this was the best sound he could get. He was doing his records justice, honoring the bands with a plinth and platter worthy of their blood and their sweat.

When the Plasmatics were booked to play on the south side of San Francisco in an old sports stadium whose main features were basketball games, Eric and Clark, with tickets, stood in line to get in. Midnight came. The doors still hadn't opened. People were pissed. Somebody threw a metal chair through a plate glass window. People rushed through the hole in the window and there they were, the Plasmatics, waiting. They were like, *If these pussies can't break into the place to see us, fuck 'em!*

Once folks had rushed the floor the Plasmatics started in with "Butcher Baby," huge bouncers holding the crowd back with plywood sheets. It was so packed in there that Eric found himself clawing people to get his head above it all for some air.

After each song Wendy O disappeared for a second then jumped back out with yet another outfit barely covering her body and sometimes her outfit *didn't* cover her at all. It was shocking, weird. As Wendy grabbed her crotch, slinging her titties around, Eric fought his way up close to the stage, and that's when Wendy O started handing Eric these things, even the skin off the bass drum that said PLAS-MATICS on it. As with all the other items she gave him— a flower, a piece of clothing that Eric assumed were her panties—the crowd pounced on him, ripping it out of his hands. The flower and panties were gone, and the prized skin.

Wendy O had seen Eric clawing to get air and Eric had felt a special connection with her.

Alas Eric's dad sold the house in the cul-de-sac off Berryessa Street. The family—Eric's mom, his dad and Eric's little brother Alain—drove over to sunny Florida, leaving Clark in California to get on with his life. Arriving in Tallahassee, the family moved into a hybrid living space half apartment, half hotel. On the deck outside slicked-up girls in bikinis stepped around and lounged in cots. Backed as it was against the parking lot of the Tallahassee mall, their new place to live, though temporary, was decent. They soon bought a house in the Velda Dairy neighborhood north of town. They renovated the garage so Eric could live in it. How happy Eric was to set up his B&O turntable and Bose speakers and get stoned while busting out his great music and snorting up Black Beauty powder.

Tallahassee was nice. There was a college radio station and a decent record store called the Record Bar on the corner of Pensacola Street and Ocala. Here Eric bought records by the Buzzcocks, Stiff Little Fingers, Pete Shelly, all kinds of new wave stuff like the new Roxy Music records and Orchestral Maneuvers in the Dark. Eric bought LA's Wasted Youth at the Record Bar and, when their times came, records by Angry Samoans and Suicidal Tendencies.

Eric's dad had been a Master Sergeant for the military, had been a navigator on a plane of some sort during the Korean conflict. Always gruff in his expressions of disappointment, his dad, who often could be seen in the gravel driveway staring into the engine bay of one of the family's cars, was a source of trouble for Eric, and an amusement for Eric's friends who came over to play in the band. Eric's dad's intolerance for hippies and the newer generation was expressed with curses. His hatred for Jimmy Carter, "Mr. Do Nothing President," was fun to watch. After fighting commies in Korea, Eric's dad contracted work with the military in Spain as a highly educated electronics expert who'd worked for Hewlett Packard, IBM, and every branch of the military save the Marines. When Marie was pregnant with Eric, and going into labor, Eric's dad dropped her off in the road near the hospital and said, "Get the fuck out." He was hardcore. Marital problems were guaranteed. Plus Eric's mom, known by one and all as an extremely delightful woman, was something of a neurotic freak herself. When Eric's mom gave birth to Eric, she called Eric's dad from the hospital and said, "It's a boy." Eric's dad said, "What did you expect it to be? A fucking dog?"

14.

Of Damaged Daughters

THE NAME "VINYL PUNKS" FELT GOOD in the mouth, and word got out you could dance to them. Their teenaged punk rock singer, people said, sounded off eerily with poetry to simple basslines while crunching out weird minor chords whose tones matched her dark content. Haunting was the word for them, for us—Eric on drums, me on bass, and Lucia, always dressed in black, on vocals and guitar. Her talent was obvious yet over my head. I was too immature, too self-involved to recognize in her an art-istry beyond anything we ourselves possessed. Here was one with an appreciation for words, who knew of mood and emotion and the generosity yof exposed wounds. Her chords went from epic into worlds of defeat, and though untrained in guitar, she threaded my basslines with divergent melodies. In our song, "Agent Death," each line of her refrain tapered from a high-pitched angry screech into a saddened lament:

Agent death, the knock of death it, wrinkles your skin, and wrinkles within.

It wraps your heart and squeezes tightly, and won't let go, till you survive it.

The Vinyl Punks, from Eric's perspective, were an experiment, a leftover crust from our days at SOAR when we were the Rubber Nipples then suddenly Lucia was our singer and we became Vinyl Punks, a band turning out to be more popular than Hated Youth. Not only did people enjoy dancing to Vinyl Punks, the word "Punks" was in their name, a plus for many in that "punk" was the thing to be. People could say, "Yeah, I saw the Vinyl Punks the other night," and whoever was listening would put two and two together: *Ahh, you're punk.* This new "dance," as they called it, where people flung arms and fists around, slamming into each other like borderline lunatics and sometimes creating a "pit," was not attractive to those who liked order and safety, values often contrary to the punk rock enterprise. But the consumers of punk did not have to embrace the supposed lifestyle, did they? All they had to do really was put on a Black Flag t-shirt come the weekend. Or Germs shirt or Fear shirt. Devo shirts and B52s shirts were okay, even Blondie shirts and Adam and the Ants shirts. While you were at it you could rip your pantyhose up a little or drip paint on your sneakers. Wasn't slam-dancing one more instance of guys insisting on having their way?

As Vinyl Punks we did five shows throughout '82 and in January '83 played again at Emmanuel's. The next time

Vinyl Punks played was in February, but we no longer called ourselves Vinyl Punks. We were Daughter Damage now, a change that may have nonplussed some of our growing fan base. Had Eric thought Vinyl Punks, like Little Johnnys, was too gay a name? It was soft, not hard. Or had Lucia come up with it? Though such details may be lost, we know that Lucia wanted to call the band Damaged Daughter, not Daughter Damage. We also can reasonably affirm that Hated Eric needed the name of his offshoot band to sound mean, in line with aggressive sensibilities.

During this time, number one on the top forty chart was "Man Eater," by Hall and Oates. Number two was "The Girl is Mine," by Michael Jackson and Paul McCartney.

At first the name Daughter Damage struck me as easier than Vinyl Punks, less original. I didn't ponder it. I accepted it, thinking our new name claimed we were out to damage the daughters of the world, or approved of the damaging of daughters. Knowing Eric, seemed possible. Or it was a statement of fact. Daughters were damaged, it would be silly to try and deny it. By their mothers, dads, teachers, uncles, employers. A daughter gets a job, say, working in the kitchen of a sandwich shop. While putting together a Reuben, hold the sauerkraut, for a paying customer, the boss's dad moseys in and puts his hand on her shoulder. "You're doing just fine," he says. She's trying to arrange the corned beef on the slice of pumpernickel, but no, the boss's dad slides his hand down her back and gives her ass a nice little squeeze. The narrative was known, all this stuff about how men did shit to make women feel small, and smaller. Then, of course, you had your handsome stranger like Ted Bundy, the kind of guy who might compliment your taste in jewelry one minute, the next take a big fat bite out of your breast. It would seem that just being born female into a patriarchy could be called a form of damage. The push for an Equal Rights Amendment had failed. Wage inequality was an issue covered often in the news. In this way our name had feminist overtones, so sure, call us *DAUGHTER DAMAGE* and call it a day. Our name was very Lucia. *She* was the damaged one. *She* was the one yet to be damaged more, mutant offspring of the comfortable, a danger even to herself. Her songs and poetry wove backwards through a mutilated web of damages.

Our new name ushered in a new member, another damaged daughter who lived in a rented house off Miccosukee Road, right down the hill from Leon High. Meet Amy Pike, same Amy of the Three Musketeer Punk Rock Girls, a graduate of Rickard's High. Amy roomed with a friend and some guys on the bottom floor while Greg and Neil from Sector 4 lived upstairs. As Amy had always liked animals, she kept rats in an aquarium that she let out now and then so they could run around her room. Rats were much easier to keep than big cats or dogs.

The Story of Amy

One day Eric came to her door. He knocked. She opened, a bloody sewing needle stuck through her nose. The sight freaked Eric out, but when Amy mentioned her Casio Tone, a foot-long plastic keyboard with buttons instead of keys, Eric asked did she want to join the band. Amy's head was newly shaved. She looked off and weird and interesting and punk. She said yes.

Daughter Damage's first show was at Smitty's, the place in the countryside out Bannerman Road. Amy held the Casio up by her neck and shoulder, swaying and treating the toy instrument as she would a violin.

Amy loved playing with the band and had a little black tunic she liked to wear during practice. She wore fishnet stockings and Chinese espadrilles.

Amy had no car, so Eric picked her up for band practice. On the drive out to the Velda Dairy neighborhood, where they rehearsed, there would be six or seven people, roiling in the oils and smells of themselves, packed into the small car. One afternoon, speeding past a school bus, somebody threw a book out the window and the book landed on the hood of Le Voiture. Eric became enraged and pulled over in front of the bus, causing it to stop. He jumped out of the car with a miniature baseball bat and ran up onto the bus with it. "Who threw the fucking book! Which one of you did it?" he shouted, pointing the bat at the terrified little kids. Everybody in the bus was screaming.

I happened to be in the trunk at the time, which was in the front of the car, under the hood, a *frunk* it was called. When I jumped out with the insane mohawks and the kids saw that, they screamed anew. For Amy, the scene was like something from the *Road Warrior* movie, just hilarious but also frightening

Eric hopped back in the car, I climbed back into the frunk, and off we drove before the cops arrived.

Daughter Damage did more shows at Smitty's, always with Hated Youth. One night somebody filmed the show. Another night Eric said to Amy, "Lucia's too drunk to sing, you'll have to sing instead," as though Amy could magically divine Lucia's lyrics, lyrics that to Amy sounded inchoate, like various emotions expressed through screams, anger, yearning, lust, self-pity. How ludicrous! Amy said no, and Daughter Damage did not play that night. Another night Amy tried wearing a zebra pattern instead of the little black tunic. Eric said, "Nope, nope, we're not having that," and made Amy change back into the little black tunic.

Lucia had stage fright. She would drink to ease through the transition from girl in the bar to superstar. Amy admired Lucia. Sometimes they went to the mall for clove cigarettes and eggrolls. For money, Amy worked at Long John Silver's as a cashier. She rode her Raleigh ten-speed to work. From Long John Silver's she graduated to Western Sizzlin' where her job was to put salad dressing on iceberg lettuce. Later, after the band broke up, she would work at Shoney's where they made her wear a wig.

Lucia always was fashionable. She always wore very white ankle socks, or crew socks, a detail she insisted on. Amy took after Lucia. For the rest of her life she would always make sure that her socks were super white. And Lucia's hair was always fantastic. Lucia said, "Don't use soap on your hair, just wash it with hot water." It's how she got it to stand up on top, sideburns on the sides, long curls on her cheeks, long black fingernails, and when she performed, she moved in a very spider-like way.

Daughter Damage played, finally, at Emory University in Atlanta, their last show. Things went well, but afterwards Eric wanted Amy's last clove cigarette. His bass guitar had been stolen, so maybe he deserved special consideration, but no, Amy wanted it for herself. For that, Eric kicked her not only out of the band, but out of the van she'd been driven to Atlanta in. Eric left Amy standing on the sidewalk in her little black tunic in the middle of the night, holding her Casio Tone, and drove away. Amy caught a ride back to Tallahassee with Sector 4 who had also played that night at the Coke Lounge.

15.

Out Bannerman Road

SMITTY'S WAS A JUKE JOINT about which people said, "It's way out in the fucking boonies, man." Though only twelve miles north of the Florida State Capitol, to get there you had to drive beyond the city limits and turn onto a wooded country road that unspooled into a darkness that seemed to have no end. Sometimes, to freak us out, Eric flipped off the van lights and we'd sail into pitch black. It was a terrifying, soul-stirring feeling that primed us for the night's fun.

Smitty Jr. had inherited the club from his dad, Smitty Sr., now buried in front of the building whose interior was of wood: wood floors, wood tables, wood chairs. Place had an old-timey feel. A long bar top ran the length of the room and against the wall was a battered juke box filled with old blues 45s and country classics like "Crazy" by Patsy Cline.

A back door let you onto the wooden staircase that took you down to the bathrooms and a cow field stretching south under the stars. Throughout '83 Hated Youth played often at Smitty's.

One weekend Stevie Stiletto and the Switchblades drove in from Jacksonville with their gear loaded in a U-Haul truck. Also loaded in the truck was the slender punk rock girl with short blond spiked hair, Converse sneakers and shorts worn over fishnet stockings. I'd seen her at the Slamfest and had also heard people talking about her, saying she was a band slut.

Hated Youth started their set, and of course I was nervous knowing that the band slut was out there watching us. A few songs in, when we segued into "Kill the Punks," doing the lunatic leads that made me seem mentally deranged, I leaped across the open floor space and slammed into her, knocking her flat on her back. On top of her on the wood floor, heads butting, I continued the messy intro stuff. As I rolled off her and jumped back up David Fats hit the snare four times and the chords and shouting began: *Kill a punk!*

She was Lexi.

After our set Hated Youth went into the cow field to smoke pot and drink. While thus engaged Lexi the Band Slut came down the outside stairs lit by the bulb hanging above the upper door. Her short spiked bleached hair carried light. It was like she was lit from within. Same for her skinny arms and face whose red mouth and shining eyes put me in a daze. Before stepping into the bathroom she looked our way, over at Eric and Lucia and me in the moon shadows. "She wants you," Lucia said. "You should go talk to her."

I could not have. I could only stare dreamily, admiring her perfection. It wasn't a question that I might somehow deign to encroach upon anything so amazing and beautiful and smart and wonderful. This band slut, like every other attractive girl in the world, was untouchably good. The most I could do was invade her privacy with my eyes.

Stevie Stiletto and the Switchblades started playing and we went back in the club and watched. We'd been getting fairly nice and drunk and stoned and I was on a stool along the bar, hoping Lexi was attracted to me, the guy who tackled her while playing his guitar, that she at least found me interesting. The band had already performed their punk rock cover of the hit song "Feelings" by Morris Albert. Things felt slow. The floor was empty, nothing happening. The singer sang into his microphone, maybe with passion but for me it was all very "lame," a stupid word, I know, but one I may have, back then, said a few times.

I'd had enough. I slipped off my stool. I carried the stool across the floor with me and, knowing the band slut watched, lifted it over my head and dropped it, caging the singer's face in with the mic attached to its stand. The mic slammed the guy in the face. The muscular he-man running Stiletto's sound sprung from behind the board with a Viking club. He would have clobbered me, but the floor erupted with slam dancers who got it his way. The guy still came after me but Hated Eric, ever primed for confrontation, stood between us. There was shouting, pushing. As Eric held the guy back, the band slut, from the other side of the room, leaned over and screamed, "You're just jealous!"

I wasn't good with girls. At SOAR kids talked of me behind my back, saying, "He must be a-sexual." There were all these hot girls at SOAR, many who seemed to *like* me, but I made no effort to get into their panties. It didn't mean I didn't like them back. I liked them too much. I wasn't worthy. Stevie Stiletto's singer, I would find out years later, went to the emergency room after the show and got stitches on his face, which might not have been the best thing for a front man in show business, but at least it was punk. In truth he was an awesome singer of an awesome band and what moved me to drop a stool over his head had nothing to do with his tousled hair, the tight pants and boots he wore, or even really the music. It was to impress the girl—let's blame the band slut.

Then there was the time, after Eric and Lucia broke up, when Eric consciously worked on his charm in order to get laid. Out Bannerman Road, in front of Smitty's on the horseshoe-shaped stretch of dirt between the little grave-yard and building, I and others watched Eric walk off with an elegant-looking woman with long hair, not your typical punk rock girl. Another girl was with them. They got in the woman's car together, and here's what happened:

In the car, partying, Eric kept thinking *I know who you are but can't put my finger on it*. The girl in the backseat was going on about some girl she saw kicked out of a rolling car on purpose. It had happened right in front of her and was extremely concerning. The girl kept saying how traumatizing it was to witness, like she had gotten PTSD from watching it. During this ridiculous monologue, Melissa, the hot chick Eric was gunning for, said, "You know what, that sounds like a lousy kick. The guy should've kicked her harder. She needed more velocity. If you're gonna kick the bitch out, kick her so there's little chance she'll land on the asphalt. There could always be another car coming up from behind." That was a little strange. The girl who told the story got offended. She got out of the car and then it was just the two of them nice and comfy.

Eric and Melissa continued to party, and as they partied Melissa kept dropping hints that she wasn't the most normal girl to walk the earth. Eric didn't care. He slid into action. Leaning over the center console, Melissa met him halfway. They fell into a blissful kiss, but right away something felt off. This kiss went way heavy way too quickly and was surprisingly vulgar. As was Eric's custom whenever a kiss began, his hand reached for the cunt. Instead of grabbing a nice little twat, his hand squeezed into a hardening chunk of meat. That's when he discovered the source of his weird misgivings, and right then figured out where he knew Melissa from. Melissa was Melvin, a guy Eric met before. He'd been fooled. He didn't know if he should be mad and get violent on her, or him, reclaiming his maleness, or let it slide. Eric settled with: *Fuck this shit, I'm out of here*, and went back inside Smitty's.

The shows at Smitty's were always fun, funny, unpredictable. One night Eric gave Gary a black sharpie and said, "I want you to write God on the side of my head." Gary said, "Sure" and wrote FAG in the freshly shaved sharkskin area below Eric's spiked mohawk. "There you go," Gary said, and Eric stuck his chest out in typical Eric fashion. With the word FAG on his head Eric strutted for the folks at the bar.

We were not the first non-Black pack of rascals to find out about Smitty's and enter the scene out there. In a July 5, 1973 article about Smitty's in the *Florida Flambeau*, writer Henri Cawthon quotes Smitty Sr. as having said, "Time brings about the change of the type of people that come in." In the article Cawthon speaks of young families living rent-free in shacks on Smitty's land in exchange for help with clean-up duties and running the bar. Another person, in response to a blog post decades later by someone named Ms. Moon, noted that throughout the changing times, back in Smitty's living space attached to the building, pictures of Martin Luther King Jr. could be seen on the walls, and of George Washington Carver and Frederick Douglass.

After Smitty Sr. died and had passed the torch to his son, white high school kids from Tallahassee discovered Smitty's as a place they could drink while underage. Fast forward to 1983. The long hair is gone. The bushy beards gone. Instead of dusty white women in cotton print dresses coming in, often barefoot with kids in overalls to get the cheap chicken dinners, there were girls in ripped-up shirts and heavy makeup done in styles not always easy to figure. The touchy-feelyness was gone. This new group of guys had heads shaved down to the quick and could be downright rowdy. They called themselves punks.

At Smitty's Hated Youth hosted the Gainesville bands Roach Motel, Terminal Fun, and Moral Sex. Our friends, the band Sector 4, played with Hated Youth at Smitty's on

New Year's Eve in a show that included Voodoo Idols from Tampa. The show was $2.50 in advance, if you bought your ticket at Vinyl Fever Records and Tapes, and $3.00 at the door. The music started around the same time a bomb went off inside the F.B.I. building in Manhattan. The cops came out that night and arrested some kids for underage drinking.

Those were the nights, but Hated Youth and Sector 4 played too at the 1982 Cow-chip Jam, which took place outside at Smitty's on a sunny Sunday in late May. One after the other bands from the eclectic mix of Tallahassee's music took the high stage overlooking the field behind the club where people were kicked back on blankets, Woodstock style, in the bare sun smoking cigarettes and weed. A few showgoers may have been high on LSD or shrooms. That afternoon, while the bands played, a tornado touched down in Tallahassee, tearing up trees and ripping roofs off warehouses not all that far from the Capitol building.

Then came the night spoken word artist John Giorno was set to perform. Eric had promised to swing by my place in Waverly Hills later with Jill, a college student he'd started dating, and drive us out to Smitty's for the performance.

To prepare, I grabbed up the dog shears I'd found in somebody's trash pile. Using a handheld mirror while looking into the bathroom mirror, I ran the swiveling blades up close to the edges of my mohawks, careful not to cut into the original lines. I shaved the remaining stubble with a disposable razor. A few cuts made my scalp bleed, but I went to the kitchen and cracked an egg over a bowl. I didn't drop the whole egg into it, only the whites. The yolk I dropped onto the drain in the sink, broke it with my fingers and ran the water.

I took the bowl up the hall to my mother's room—she wasn't home—and passed through her bedroom into her bathroom. I opened the cabinet. I grabbed her K-Y Jelly tube and squeezed a blob from it into the bowl, which I then took back to my room at the other end of the house. Here, in my bathroom, I swirled the mixture with my fingers then used the goop to spike my mohawks. If you used egg whites only, your mohawks could crack and drop eggy flakes all over the place. The K-Y Jelly gave your mohawks a pliant edge. If somebody brushed their hand across them, the hair would bend then bounce back to its original position.

I was ready. I could go outside now and be radical, maybe dangerous in some way in the night. But Eric and Jill were not showing up.

Why weren't they showing up?

I had looked forward to going to Smitty's, to being around Jill, too, who had said nice things to Eric about me that Eric then went and told me about. She was smart yet humble and was short enough for me to forget she was nearly twenty. But where were they? If they were running late, Eric would have called. Time kept going by and going by and they still kept not showing up.

The feeling. In my room. Of hopeful expectancy. Turned to doubt. And disbelief. Then there was no doubt. No disbelief. In my room. Where I slept. And rolled joints, put my socks on and wrote songs. This room had warped into an overturned barrel the night I drank cherry-flavored shroom Kool-Aid. Reality, then, proved unreliable. My fears manifested. Now, seeing I could not trust what my friends said, I took off my clothes and sat on the tall stool sideways to my reflection on the vertical strip of wall mirror. Defeated. My mohawks were spiked. I was alone, nobody coming to get me. Seeing myself in the mirror, one foot drawn onto the seat of the stool, the other leg dangling, I thought somebody should take a picture. I had the feeling I would never again be so perfect.

16.

Gary Gets Scary

BEFORE GARY SHOUTED SHOUTS for Hated Youth, and before Gary transferred from Leon High to the School of Analytical Reasoning, Gary took a test that established this: Gary had an SLD, or Specific Learning Disability, the specificity here being math. In an effort to fix Gary's deviation he was removed from his normal math class and put into a room filled with other SLD kids, their specific "disabilities" ranging the spectrum. One guy masturbated in the back of the room while rocking like a pigeon, drooling. At some point Gary had the thought, *I'm not like him, I think there's a difference.* Gary didn't like it. Then the lady running the show said if you complete the whole workbook, you can go back to the normal class. There was hope. The lady didn't expect Gary to complete the workbook, but he did. The lady reneged on her promise. Gary had to stay in the class. Gary felt dismal and doomed and filled with hate.

A guy named Charles lived in the John Knox apartment complex where Gary lived. Charles told Gary about SOAR, how great SOAR was, saying, "SOAR has a catfish farm!" Gary was into fish. Gary loved all things aquatic. He loved reading about Jacques Cousteau and was currently working on getting his scuba license. Gary applied to SOAR. Gary's spot on the waiting list came up. Gary was accepted—*yay!*

Next thing Gary knew Gary was in a band. Things were happening for Gary. Gary had a cute girlfriend with a soft body and, as there was an extra bedroom in the government subsidized rental where Gary lived, and since Gary's mom slept at her boyfriend's place most nights, Gary made a little money by renting the room to David, who moved in with the sparkly sense of humor he was known for, his zits and hamburger wrappers and drumsticks. One day while David was away from the apartment, Gary snooped around in David's room. Gary found magazines with naked guys in them. In David's drawer Gary found sex toys and under the bed a sawed-off broomstick. Gary pulled it out and brought it up to his nose.

Another day, when Gary was with David over at Gary's girlfriend's place, David was on the couch. The plan was for them all to go to Chuck E. Cheese, get pizza and have a great time, but while Gary was in the bathroom, getting ready, he heard David and Trudy out there talking about him. Sounded to Gary like David was talking shit on him and his blood went straight to a boil. He heard David say, "Gary cares too much about what people think about him," at which point Gary was done. He slammed out of the bathroom and ran over there and punched David square in the face.

Blood poured out of David's face.

"I'm sorry!" Gary said and went and got paper towels from the kitchen for David, saying "I'm sorry, I'm sorry."

Gary drove David and Trudy to the hospital, crying the whole way there, and when David came out of the hospital Gary hugged David, he was just really sorry, he could hardly believe he had done such a thing, but David's parents said no, David had to press charges—just look at their son's face, it was swollen something terrible, he looked battered—so David pressed charges.

Instead of arresting Gary for assault, they siphoned Gary into JASP, the Juvenile Alternative Services Project designed to help troubled teens bypass getting criminal records. You had to do twenty hours of community service, which Gary did at the Leon County Spay and Neuter Clinic—it was Gary's first time seeing a surgery performed and, seeing blood, he damn near threw up.

A burst of anger, that's what it was, or was it? It wasn't Gary's first outburst. There was the time, early on, that Gary walked across the band room, casually, and sideswiped me across the face. I sat there stunned, not knowing what I'd said or done to piss Gary off. Another time, while Gary was at home, Gary heard his sister talking with some guy on the phone. The guy was trying to date her. After the call Gary's sister told Gary that the guy said he was going to beat Gary's ass. Gary knew the guy meant this to try and sound tough in front of his sister, but brewed on it. When the guy came over later to see her, Gary acted calm, waiting all the while for the guy to show that same attitude he'd had during the phone call with his sister. As soon as he did, Gary punched him. The guy fell down so Gary kicked him and Gary was punching and kicking him and kicking and punching him. "Oh really?" Gary shouted, "You're gonna beat my ass?" It felt great!

Punishment

Over the nose thing Gary went to court: a room with an oval desk in it where decisions were made and penalties given. The guy in charge sat across the table from Gary and Gary's mom who had grown up in foster homes and an orphanage and had at one point even been a lay Carmelite who dreamed of becoming a nun. The guy said, "What's your drug of choice, Gary?" Gary didn't even drink. "None." The guy said, "Don't lie to me, Gary. I can tell by the way your eyes look that you do drugs." Gary asked the guy what he meant. The guy said, "The way they're sunken into your head like that. Listen, kid, I've been to England, capiche? I've rolled around in glass, done the whole nine yards, there's nothing you can say that will surprise me, so you might as well spit it out."

Gary had nothing to say, wasn't much he could do here, so he went along with it, participated in the plan.

Part of the guy's job was to pick Gary up from SOAR along with another kid who'd gotten in trouble. From SOAR the guy drove the kids over to Leon High, picked up another delinquent and drove them home. That's all he was supposed to do, drive them home, but then Gary starts hearing the guy talking code language to the other kids. The guy sounded like their drug dealer. What the guy had wanted, when asking Gary what kinds of drugs he used, was the opportunity to dock more dollars. Some kind of counselor, this guy. The kids in the program were his hookup for selling drugs.

Gary's girlfriend moved in once David moved out. But the Astoria Arms was infested with roaches. Gary learned the differences between female and male roaches. The females are wider. When Gary couldn't see them, he smelled them. It was a subtle sweet smell like an old dried-up nugget of brown sugar. Gary hated it. Trudy didn't like it either so, to get away from the roaches, they moved to a nicer place called London Town.

17.

Just Shutup Already!

COME JUNE OF '83, on the 10th and 16th, Hated Youth played Gainesville at a spot called the Spot, the first time with Roach Motel and Terminal Fun, then with Roach Motel and Channel 3 whose song, "I've Got a Gun," for whatever reason—maybe because it evoked the style of the Clash—was aired in a video on MTV. After that Hated Youth zipped over to Jacksonville to headline for the Wads from Saint Augustine. On the way there, closing in on the venue, Gary said, "My dick gets hard whenever we get closer to the show. Does that ever happen to you?" Eric laughed in mounting crescendo, a fully felt *heh heh heh* that encouraged that kind of talk, which I didn't much care for. Any talk of dicks and buttholes and pubic hairs cringed me out. They were having their moment of male bonhomie but in my mind I was like *Shutup already*.

The Wads show was in a shoebox of a restaurant sort of Hispanic niche, the vibe dark, humorless skinheads in dirty white t-shirts hanging out front in the sunlight and there was a general sense of crime and danger, a brewing menace about which the Wads seemed unfazed. For the drummer of the Wads, also leader of the band, was built. His only concern was getting his cymbals set up right as he now and then sipped from his water bottle. Though he may have been tough, he looked funny in his bodybuilding shirt. The sweatband worn around flybacks gave him an almost disco look. He was a mix between Leif Garret and the flamboyant exercise guru, Richard Simmons, so these skinheads had better not cause any trouble, not while the Wads played.

The Wads, though, were not hardcore. Their music did not inspire violence. They made it through their set fine. Not until Hated Youth started up did the skinheads, who seemed Hispanic or something, like maybe they were Cubans, I don't know, go berserk, grabbing up tables and throwing them. They smashed pasta plates and jabbed forks into the wall. The shocked and pissed off owner broke into the ruckus to shut shit down.

The thing about shit getting shut down was not new to Hated Youth. Our first show, as the Little Johnnys, was even cancelled; *that* time it was for, as word had it, an item published by Christopher Farrell of the Speed Queens (the intended headliner) that slammed a major radio station's LP release of local bands. The album, *D-103 Tallahassee's Hottest*, included longtime local faves such as John Kurzweg & the Night, the Know-It-Alls, Benny Jones, Eli and Crosscut Saw. The show had been scheduled to go down at the Seminole Reservation on Lake Bradford. Upon hearing that it was cancelled, Farrell phoned Reel Rock productions, a company that would deliver and assemble a PA system for you for $150. The bands each chipped in and the show, or at least the punk part of the show, was moved to *the Green*.

Hated Youth got shut down in Waverly Hills, too, where we played in my garage at 707 Lothian Drive, the noise of us, or music, if you will, invading the spaces of neighbors who may have been reading the *Tallahassee Democrat*, catching the latest on Israel's bloody campaign against the Muslims, trying to watch *Star Trek* on TV, perhaps, or heating up soup by microwave. Whatever the case, cops came out to shut us up, same as it was when we played the Jerry Lewis Labor Day Telethon at the Tallahassee mall, and same as it was and would be in other shows in other places yet to come. Our unspoken assumption as punks was we were above it. Whoever didn't like our intrusions should go ahead and pour Drāno into their earholes.

And just shutup already.

"Shutup!" my mother said to me when I was a tiny little baby, and I guess I don't blame her, I mean, imagine if you were what people considered a beautiful young woman, and you had long silky hair and were also what people, yourself included, considered multitalented and smart. Suddenly there's this whimpering sniffling diaper-shitting mutant creature begging for milk and attention as you're trying to learn a classical guitar song so that other people, once you've got it down good, can watch you perform it and swoon over how amazing you are. Wouldn't it piss you off too? Wouldn't you hiss, "Shutup!" and then hit STOP on the tape recorder, put the guitar down roughly, grab the damn thing up and shove the feeder in its mouth?

Of course you would.

Following our Wadly misadventure in Jacksonville, on a Thursday in October in Gainesville, Hated Youth played with Roach Motel and Beyond Therapy (the new name for Terminal Fun, John McQuiggins still presiding on vocals) at the Late Nite Bottle Club. Was Reagan threatening Russia? Was Reagan telling Russia to stop helping Syria help Lebanon? We didn't care. Of whatever was going on in faraway lands, we were ignorant. If you asked Eric or I or Gary or David where Syria was, we would not have been able to say.

Just shutup already.

We stayed the night at Roach Motel drummer Frank Mullen's place and in the morning met up with John McQuiggins who'd slept at somebody else's house even though he lived in Gainesville. McQuiggins and his bassist were sitting cross-legged on the floor with their electric instruments and playing songs, unamplified, by the Cure, a band they seemed to take as superior, somehow, to Florida's newly foliating hardcore punk scene, a view I found puzzling. Though I knew nothing of the Cure, I knew they were mainstream. That alone made them despicable. It was odd. How could you like something mainstream (Devo and the B52s had long ago lost their appeal) while at the same time writing elemental songs of anger concerned with getting the lead out, saying something in your face, indulging in purposeful ignorance or taking verbal revenge on the assholes, aka adults, in charge? Here my contemporaries exalted the Cure, and the reason for it, I gathered, was the Cure might have seemed more intelligent lyrically, more advanced musically, and perhaps even the dark eye shadow had a draw. To me, it was but a step sideways of Boy George whose band, the Culture Club, was #1 right then in the U.K. with their song, "Karma Chameleon."

At some point the guy in charge of the place McQuiggins had stayed the night got onto McQuiggins over a long-distance phone bill he'd rung up while talking to Lexi the Band Slut in Jacksonville. Apparently McQuiggins, unlike me, had had some luck with her. We were about to go, but McQuiggins said he wouldn't mind hopping along to Miami with us. Eric said, "Hell yeah, let's go, Quiggy boy."

In this way we set out in the direction of Miami, McQuiggins shotgun while Gary and Trudy and I were crammed into the back with all the equipment, Gary and Trudy in a tiny little vestibule at the very back of the van, in the rear, as it were. Gary and Trudy could net even look out of the back windows, and sitting on the metal floor, not able to be a part of conversations and stuff that were happening on the other side of the equipment, Gary seethed. He felt silenced, as though he had no status in the band. Here McQuiggins wasn't even scheduled to play, he was along for the ride yet look at him up there with a front row seat?

Me, I had a cramped space in the middle of the van, but was like *Okay, I'll hang out here until Miami, no biggy.* I was crammed between the components of Eric's Earth amplifier and my puffy Kustom with the intensity and reverb switches.

We arrived in Miami ahead of time for our show of October 21, 1983. The place was called Flynn's Ocean 71. With us on the bill were Broken Talent and D.A.M. A girl who worked for the club invited us into an elevator whose door, when it reached the top floor, slid back to reveal a regular door with a doorknob. She opened it and we followed her into what looked like a large maintenance room where people had thrown extra paint cans and cleansing liquids in jugs.

Gary and Trudy stayed in a different room that Trudy paid for with her credit card, a place she and Gary could be away from things and fuck around and do what they wanted before the show started. After checking in they checked out the neighborhood, surprised to find vending machines selling newspapers written only in Spanish. It was like they had entered a whole new world.

Returning to the club, Gary and Trudy met a cool punk couple that lived in the hotel. I met them too. The guy was decked out in the punk style and their room was spray-painted with slogans, the main one being CHAOS, a word I was familiar with, but not sure about, like what did it really mean? How do you pronounce it? The word was the second word in the name of a band the guy dreamed of one day forming, a band he was going to call Social Chaos.

This guy and the empty beer cans all over and the punk girlfriend made a strong impression. Within his exuberant talk the name Nietzsche popped out several times, a name I had never heard even though my dad knew by heart every one of Nietzsche's books and had explained Nietzsche's ideas in detail to classrooms filled with philosophy and political science students. He'd even taught Nietzsche to my mother when she was his student up north, before they married, wooing her with radical ideas about human parasites and changing the world for the better.

Well, my dad stood nothing to gain by telling *me* of Nietzsche. I had no titties, nor no hot wet dripping pussy, two items that had been prime motivators throughout his life. As a master cynic, sharing "pearls" with his competition—yes, all his sons took away time and devotion from his wife that should have been dedicated to him alone—made no sense. What did make sense was to get the little fuckers to shutup as much as possible, a logical position that his wife made every effort to enforce. In this way I became extremely skilled at moving across floors soundlessly. For fun, and to test my skills, I walked barefoot over smashed glass and leafy ground, no crunch sounds coming out of me, no peeps. My earliest memories include watching the 6 o'clock news in our family room, seeing bombs fall out of airplanes flying over Vietnam, creating great explosions and fires in the jungles below. Whenever I tried to say something, like ask a question about the guys seen setting thatched huts on fire with flamethrowers, his wife always jumped in with a threatening "Shh!"

Just shut the fuck up already!

This punk guy said Nietzsche is where Hitler got his idea for "the superman." I was dumbfounded and interested. Punk posters were on their walls. They were like Sid and Nancy, a British feel in their presentation. Another item of interest was the guy had tuned his guitar to an open G because he didn't have the skill to play regular bar chords. Neither Gary nor I had seen that before, and Gary thought it was really cool that you could play chords up and down the neck with one finger.

Broken Talent played, then D.A.M (Don't Ask Me) played. Then Hated Youth was up on the high stage. Someone with a microphone out there in the dim light by the soundboard, probably Richard Shelter, who ran the club, went, "Ladies and gentlemen, all the way from Tallahassee, what you've been waiting for, Hated Youth!" and right then David hit his sticks together. The lights flipped on and we fell into it, Gary screaming "I wanna join the KKK" and me running out onto the bar top attached to the stage whose topography of ashtrays and beer bottles I disturbed only minimally. We gave the audience what we had to give.

But the people scared Gary shitless. Those people out there had mohawks and spikes in their jackets and the women looked interesting and available. Even the décor intimidated. The blood-colored walls were decked with framed images of obscure material while above us professional theater lights flashed all colors of the rainbow, the ceiling a warped mirror image of our split-level stage shaped after a gigantic piano. Wires ran haywire over our heads, and below us was another network of tangles dedicated to maintaining our sound, to making people hear us in this glorious presentation of shifting color. On the wall, stage left, an American flag was draped neatly in a minefield of mirrors sporting badges of beers. At one point, a guy ran through the crowd straight at Gary and managed to get his foot up on the top of the stage. The guy did a back flip into the human sea behind him. All those people out there, those strangers. There was no way to know what they might do. This extra jab of adrenaline made Gary lean into his performance with unrestrained aggression.

After the show, Gary and Trudy sat in the club. Trudy got up to use the bathroom. A girl came over and flopped down beside Gary. She said she published a fanzine. She was trying to talk, maybe to write something about Hated Youth, but Gary was afraid. He didn't want Trudy to come back and see them together. She would flip out. So he wasn't very talkative. The girl jumped up suddenly out of nowhere and said, "Fuck you!" and walked away.

In the morning we did breakfast at McDonald's, one of my favorite things to do after a night with the band, a reward, if you will. I loved sauntering in through the glass doors where all was shiny and glowed from the morning light pouring in, and where people of all creeds, some with children, others dropping in on their way to work, gassed up for the day. We'd order our stuff and splurge on these Styrofoam combo plates of eggs and sausage that included, *da dant dah dah*: three pancakes with butter and syrup! Cutting into those golden cakes with a plastic fork, I felt independent, like an adult, like somebody you might see across a room and think, *Oh, he's one of us.*

We drove home and that night, a little after midnight, two suicide bombers in another part of the world detonated their trucks loaded with thousands of pounds of explosives, hello Islamic Jihad. The blasts, which happened at the U.S. and French embassies in Beirut, permanently silenced hundreds of Marines and military people. *Shutup! Shutup! Shutup and shalom!* This was the lovesome and evolved people-care-about-each-other world we lived in, hey hey.

18.

Postbellum Walkabout

HATED YOUTH'S SECOND AND FINAL Atlanta act was at the Metroplex on Luckie Street with DDT, also the abbreviation, somebody explained, for a toxic pesticide that had got into the food chain, making people lose control over their bodies and minds, their lungs screwed up and their skin. We arrived early. After setting up we explored, walked down Marietta Street to Forsyth Street where I climbed onto a statue. I was in my white t-shirt with a red cross on it crossed out in black. I had made the strikethrough symbol using cardboard stencils, the edges sharp. It had a printed look as much as a spray-painted look. I was trying to look interesting, I guess, never mind that I was stating the obvious.

Still, it pissed people off. "Your mother ought to be ashamed of you," I heard, and "How dare you?" It simply was inconceivable to me that anybody could believe such things. And to think that people killed each other over it, that to slaughter some Muslim punk coming over the hill, or Jewish punk, depending on which side you were on, was an act of heroism. Just pick up a Bible. Thumb through it, reading snatches as you go. You'll see bloodshed in big numbers going back thousands of years. In Anno Domini 1983 the same was true. Flip on the TV. See the hate, the hatred, the hateful taking up of sides. And so ban it, the Bible, and ban the Quran. Band them together with every screed squeaking of alliances with deities instead of between peoples. Drag the fuckers with their little books and specialized garb into the stadiums and set upon them your sleuths of starving grizzly bears. Sit back and watch. Will God even once, like He did with Daniel, lift a finger to stop the beasts from sinking teeth into these heathens of life and living? While at it, goad the CEOS of tobacco empires out there along with the guy who invented the low battery warning chirp for smoke alarms. Let the carnage go down to some Verbal Assault or Corrosion of Conformity.

At least Jesus, they say, said, "Forgive them, Father, for they know not what they do." He also seemed to sort of tell his mom to fuck off when she came to him while he was dying on the cross.

I had a camera with me—a Pentax K-1000, property of the School of Analytical Reasoning. Before climbing onto the statue, I gave it over to Eric who shot me in the lap of the woman figure at the memorial honoring Henry Grady, a long dead Southern politician who told violent racial jokes publicly and argued for legislation guaranteed to ensure forever "the supremacy of the white race of the South." The statue whose lap I was in was of a robed woman with a scroll in her hand and book under her bare foot. We did not know what Grady stood for, but looking at the woman whose lap I was in one might guess *Grady and company* were convinced of the righteousness of their cause and were intent on making it stick by means of learning and an administration of "justice" through law. The inscription at the memorial revealed that Grady died in 1889.

Atlanta was a thrill.

And Lucia Cartledge even lived here. After breaking up with Eric, Daughter Damage over and done with, she came and melded with Atlanta's punk scene. We knew she might come to the show, and she did. She stepped in with a friend, both wearing black spandex leggings, Lucia's presentation free of constraint: bright shiny lipstick on her, heavy makeup, big black hair and a tight black shirt studded with punk pins. She spoke with Eric for a few minutes, suggesting, he would tell me later, that he go off with her and her friend and the three could have sex together. Who knows. She and her friend stayed for a few Hated Youth songs then left while we were playing. Within the year she would marry the guitarist for the Razor Boys, change her name to Lucia O'cia Svelte Razor and hang out and party with musicians who came through town doing shows, people like Stiv Bators and Iggy Pop.

After we played two girls came up to me and Gary, one with light hair, the other's hair dark. Maybe they were friends. They complimented us on the show and the one with light hair held her hand my way. I put my hand in hers and my god it was warm. I was humbled by her attention, made still. What was I to do? My face turned pink, I'm sure, for she was not off the map of the conceivable. She was a comfortable sight, a "girl" so different from, for example, the "girl" I saw step up from the curb in front of the Spot the night we played in Gainesville with Channel 3—*that* girl, or call her a woman if you'd rather, had walked by the people standing out front with a frolicsome gait that made everybody look whether they wanted to or not. She wore tight jeans, was maybe a college student, and her painfully thin t-shirt was such that the contours of her young breasts were on full display, unconscientiously in the lead, not pulling the girl proper along behind them, but being propelled forward by the acting entity, their boss whose perfect body and unmarred beautiful face revealed a haughtiness and sense of self-possession and grandeur that made me recoil. She was attractive. That was the problem in that otherwise she was repulsive. She seemed to personify the source of all human suffering.

Gary and Trudy that night drove to Marietta where Trudy's family had a house. Eric and David and I stayed at the Metroplex, each of us finding a spot on the floor and closing our eyes for an hour or two of dream. Early in the morning, once it was light out yet the streets were still empty and quiet, we skateboarded the slope of Luckie Street.

Shortly after Atlanta we started rehearsing on Branch Street where Eric lived with his new girlfriend. Because punk rock and hardcore were still relatively new features of the Tallahassee music scene, a film crew came out from FSU one afternoon for footage of us playing in our cramped band space of the scrawled-on walls.

This was for a closed-circuit TV production about punk rock and hardcore, an informative treat for the college kids kicking back in their dorms. It began with a clip of the

Slut Boys playing "God Save the Queen." The history of punk, how it supposedly grew out of working-class discontent in England is hit upon, and we also have a Slut Boy wearing dark sunglasses sitting on a couch. Like a true rock star he says that punk rock was basically already dead when it washed up on our shores in 1977.

The student reporters visit Tennessee Street to see what people hanging out in front of the clubs of a Friday night think about punk rock. Does it even still exist? "Punk does everything everyone else is afraid to do," says one young neatly groomed stud with an aristocratic-sounding Southern accent. Except for the earring, he looks like one of the gentlemen wearing colorful suits and bowties in the scene from *Gone With the Wind* where the men get in a tizzy over Clark Gable warning that the Yanks are in a better position to dominate in a war. Another young man, also of Southern stock, says, "The motivating force behind the music is to change, not be the same, do something new and unique and don't get stuck in the same rut," a notion buttressed by a guy in his forties with a Boston accent who says, "It's the hippies all over again, it's the greasers from my era all over again, this stuff keeps coming back and there's nothing new here except spiked hair."

Hated Eric, in his comments, appears to agree with the older guy. Wearing a flannel shirt buttoned to the neck, he says, "Hardcore is just like basic rock and roll all over again, except this time they just upbeated it again." As to hardcore's supposed uncertain status in American culture, or at least Tallahasseean culture, where less than a hundred and twenty years before the cotton fields on the outskirts of town teemed with slaves in osnaburg breeches and sack dresses, he says, "Hardcore is an acquired taste, it's like scotch. You can't just jump into it and say okay, I like this."

We ourselves did not see the production until forty years later when a local music junkie, someone who'd been in the band Gothic Playground that had formed in Tallahassee around the time Hated Youth broke up, went to some pains to disinter the footage. Though there might be a few extant clips of us out there somewhere in the world, these are the only moving pictures we've seen of Hated Youth.

Alas an afternoon came when, upon gathering for practice on Branch Street, the subject arose that maybe Hated Youth should call it quits. Why not? High school was ending. I had been accepted into the Southeast Center for Photographic Studies in Daytona Beach, where I was to start college in September, and Eric planned to go to California with his girlfriend after she graduated from FSU and start a new band there. Why continue? We didn't always get along, did we? There were times that David went MIA and was hard to get in touch with—he was hanging out with a biker gang, we later found out, exploring his sexuality—and hadn't Gary once cracked David's nose bone in half?

Sure, those could serve as reasons enough to quit, but more likely our circle of musical comradery broke over Eric's becoming increasingly frustrated by what he could not do on the bass, stuff I tried getting him to do. I did not complain of his bass-playing, that I recall, but maybe he was slowing us down. Maybe he felt humiliated by the fact that I had had to play the bassline for our song "JFA" when we went to Mirror Image Studio in Gainesville to record tracks for our intended release of an album we hoped to call *Hardcore Rules*. Eric saw that he wasn't growing musically, that he was below par in an activity that required great precision, and besides that, his bent was for the light—he wanted to be out there with the voice, daunting and dazzling as he owned the stage like a Jello, Milo, Henry or H.R.

My own opinion on Eric's bass playing skills—and you can check out his picking on the recordings of us—is they were good enough, certainly as good as if not better than pimple-faced Sid Vicious's ever were. The problem was we already played a thousand times faster than the Sex Pistols. We were faster than anything that had thus far come out of the UK. We were "upbeated" to the max. The trajectory of what we were doing indicated that this quality was only going to intensify in the future, and that already we were having to hold off vast new worlds of compelling complexity. I wanted to expand, explore, get into the nitty-gritty of things like other bands seemed to do, but we kept our approach basic. In essence we were in a rut.

But maybe I'm not being fully honest. The crux of it may have been this: with Eric you weren't supposed to have much of a mind of your own, not if you were close to him, and he really did suffer from jealousy, which was a side of his character that he made no effort to conceal. Seeing others being better at him at anything, whether it be happiness, skateboarding, getting attention, playing a beautiful lick on an instrument—it didn't matter what—caused him distress that he acted on to try and alleviate, and the best way to alleviate such stress was to make an effort to drag down the offending item, stomp it out, belittle it, hamper it from achieving more of the same feeling in him or, if a tangible item was involved, take it. When he tore up Lucia's French cigarettes, it wasn't because he cared about her health. It was because he didn't like seeing her be *too* cool. Just how dare she be svelte and shiny. How dare she look contented and take on the qualities of a starlet on the silver screen. When Eric drop kicked me at Murphy's house show, it was for the admiration he saw directed my way, instead of his. Eric was the kind of guy who, if he saw you with a nice new pair of sneakers, he would step on them and smear them with dirt, all with a smile, of course, an in-your-face declaration that he was the boss of things, that you might as well quit trying to be awesome because he would always be there to ruin it. "I'm breaking them in for you," he'd say. Being on top was a major part of his personality, so when it came to being a weak link in the band, he may have seen only two options: catch up with John and David, which seemed out of reach at this point, or call things off.

I accepted our new status as a broken-up band, agreed even that it was the right thing. Goodbye everybody! Let the runt puppy die curled up in its little corner. Let's walk on through the sparkling post-bellum paradise that is our home. A week or two later, though, Eric went over to Gary's place in London Town to say Hated Youth reformed without him—*What?*—that Eric sang now—how else could it have gone?—and that a long-haired country boy named Tommy did bass.

19.

Backyard Hardcore Skate Party

HATED YOUTH'S BADASS HAIRY NEW BASSIST played with Hated Youth for the first time in the backyard of the house Eric rented with Brooke, a business major delighted by the contrast she and Eric projected as a couple, a beauty-and-the-beast dynamic that highlighted Brooke's winning qualities. While Brooke could have been a model for Victoria's Secret and wore conservative clothes and had the poise of an intellectual, not to mention great tan, Eric, known universally now as *Hated* Eric, was a high school dropout who painted houses to support his band and buy weed. Of Eric people said his body was a bit overly odiferous, a bit much to bear while having him in the house with you—we had even once considered calling ourselves the Violent Odors—whereas Brooke smelled of wild roses and forest rain.

The flyers for the show that we stapled to phone poles all up and down Tennessee Street, as was our custom, advertised a "Back to School Hardcore Skate Party" and gave the time and address: 9:00 PM at 1316 Branch Street between 6th and 7th Avenues. Thing was, we had no halfpipe. Who cared? Eric simply loaded a pack of skaters into the Centel van, a van revered amongst the skaters for its previous contributions to the SKATE OR DIE cause. Eric drove the crew through upscale neighborhoods into newly developing areas—that's where the wood was! At these construction sites 2x4s and stacks of 4x8 plywood sat out front like wildflowers begging for somebody to come along and pick. Hated Youth even had a song about that van. It went, "Eric's van is so damn bad!"

The guy Eric bought the van from had switched its straight-six out with a Windsor 351, an engine so large it barely fit the bay. Eric could smoke his tires from Spot A to wherever he wanted Spot B to be. As a result of the oversized engine, the exhaust manifold pressed against the steel cover that would start to glow red in places. It would melt the rubber soles off your shoes.

Eric's van was a great van, true to the song, but had issues. Earlier that year, in January, driving to the Channel 3 show in Gainesville, the radiator hose blew out, causing the engine cover, or doghouse, as it was also called, to crack back violently. Only Eric and David were in the van, along with Hated Youth's amplifiers and drums and other loose ends of equipment. They pulled over. On exposing the engine, both were splashed in the face with hot radiator fluid. Already they were late for the show. They were close enough though to try to rig things. Eric taped the hose with duct tape. He and David filled whatever jugs and buckets they could find with water from a nearby ditch and drove along the highway with the engine cover off, David pouring water into the radiator so they wouldn't run hot. As they approached the show venue, there was Zilpha, our manager's girlfriend, waving her arms, crying, "You're late, you're late!" The woman wouldn't get out of the way so Eric drove straight at her, damn near plowed her over. Because Eric and David were so late getting to the show, Hated Youth played that night as headliners, not openers, for a nationally known band whose video played on MTV.

Eric and the skaters anyway were on the hunt in the edges of the city. A golden stack popped up. Eric steered into the site. Parked. The skaters piled out with tinsnips and screwdrivers for the stacks in steel bands. They were making progress. They were loading the van with wood but then some guy shows up and shouts, "Hey!" That's all Eric needed. He jumped over the plywood pile and shot into the driver's seat like a caped superhero. "Hold on kids!" he cried, and hit the pedal, one of the blond-haired skater boys flinging out into the air while holding onto the door that hadn't yet been shut. Doing a rooster tail out of the construction site, Eric saw the kid in his side mirror jerking around back there like a cartoon ragdoll.

It wasn't enough wood, but the skater boys made do. They built the halfpipe the day before the show. It was crude, had only one platform. They spray-painted it up with cool slogans from hardcore albums and called it a day.

Folks showed up around eight the following evening. They milled about while skaters skated and Eric in the house had sex with Brooke and snorted cocaine. "I put some in her cunt," he said, coming down from the house.

Eric's excuse for not skating was his "hipper," what he got the day before after falling off his board on the new ramp. He even went to the ER thinking he'd broken a bone or had torn something important inside of his butt. Turned out to be a nope, no, and a no sir, all he had was the hipper, a regular ole everyday hipper. Eric and the board, same as it was for Eric and the bass, were not great friends. Eric therefore limped and used a cane tonight, though he watched me having a blast on the new ramp. I had learned how to rock and roll. I grinded the PCV coping and pulled off small airs, backside and frontside. I couldn't get enough of that ramp.

Hated Youth's opening band was Xband, the band Tommy, our great new sasquatch bass player, played guitar in. As Xband played the skaters skated back and forth, up and down and backwards and around, doing the fakey and carving. It all was great fun until a skater flew over the drop-in platform and broke his neck. An ambulance came and hauled him away. It bummed us out but we had a set to do. We picked up our instruments and fell into it, busting out our new song, "Take the Baby and Run."

Our new bassist could play anything and everything. There was no stumbling along the way as it had been with Eric. Our slag time was now at about zero, no need to practice much, even, just play, we had it. It freed me up to write songs and I wrote lots. Eric wrote bunches too, "No Good," and "I'm Sick of It" that went "I'm sick and tired of my life, but it's my life. Don't tell me what the fuck to do, cuz it's my life." The songs practically wrote themselves, combusting spontaneously whenever we flipped on the amps. We were like a medium for something else happening. This was no let's sit down and perfect shit huddling together of musicians—nope, nothing precious here, nothing Beatles. As soon as I busted out the riffs, Tommy had them down, every song killer.

Hated Youth plays Branch Street, Eric's first time as lead singer

The one I wrote about stealing off with a woman's baby, torturing the damn thing then eating it, was inspired by a private moment shared with the bassist for Terminal Fun. During the Florida Slamfest in Gainesville, he and I walked off to get burgers. In front of Wendy's was this baby in a stroller, its mom inside ordering stuff, I don't know what, hamburgers, French fries, a chocolate frosty, whatever. Terminal Fun's bassist—a lanky guy named Greg or Craig—said, "Man, we should grab that baby and haul ass." Seemed like a cool and wild and crazy thing to do, like really we maybe might ought to do that, so I wrote a song about it. The song had a slow part *and* a fast part, which was the trend in all the great new music coming out. The starting lyrics, during the slow part, went:

It's a sad sad story, it's about a lady, somebody stole her baby. Well me and Dave, we were out one night, we came across the most beautiful sight. Someone left their baby in a shopping cart to steal. Well me and Dave took advantage of that, we took it home for a meal. We played with its toes, we chopped off its nose, we used its throat for a garden hose. We shaved it bald, stuck an apple in its mouth, set in in the oven and put it to roast.

I could write anything I wanted, so why not tell the truth? Anybody could see there were too many babies. Anybody could see how making babies was at its core a rotten thing to do and that in a perfect world the perpetrators would be punished, strung up in town squares across the country to be publicly used and abused by the Birth Police. Having babies was the worst form of terrorism, was worse even than smoking cigarettes—what an irresponsible messed-up thing to do! Writing songs about stuff like that, psychological tensions stored in your body could be released. I mean, think if Craig or Greg and I actually ran off with the thing. Not that we'd stuff it in a blender then turn the blender on mince, like I wrote about in the song, but who knew where such wild dangerous thoughts could lead you? Though we may have felt open to getting in big trouble, in our hearts we didn't want to get entangled with the law. Better to write songs about the stupid shit going on around you. Nobody gets hurt. I wrote of my fears, like doing drugs until my brain exploded, was fried, and it was *too late* for me to save myself. All those drugs got to me, didn't they? Well, at least I didn't grow breasts as the school authorities promised I would if I smoked pot.

In the new songs rats ate my face, dogs bit me. I got rabies. I killed my mother with a golf club (sorry, Mom), and Eric and David and Tommy and I busted open the side doors of Eric's van to gun down our fans: "Machine gun 'em down!" Eric screamed seven times in a row, like this: "Machine gun 'em down! Machine gun 'em down! Machine gun 'em down! Machine gun 'em down! Machine gun 'em down! Machine gun 'em down! Machine gun 'em down now!!"

We called that one "S.O.S." It was no reference to the distress code meaning "Save Our Souls." No, our "S.O.S." stood for Social Obliteration Squad. That's what we were! In this pre-Columbine death fantasy we planted time bombs and threw grenades. It was the sister song to our song, "Gainesville Massacre," which included the line, "They follow each other, it's a brotherhood."

We had a loner sensibility going on, even though we were a "group," and in Eric's masterpiece, "Loner," our most melodic song—Eric came dangerously close to what might be called "singing" instead of "shouting"—he sang: "I'll live my life, and you live yours, I'll say it isn't nothing, and you say yours, cuz I'm doing all right, by myself, if you need someone, go someplace else." And then the chorus: "Leave me alone, blow away, don't come back another fucking day, cuz I'm doing all right, by myself, if you need someone, go to hell!"

Brutal!

Other new Eric-songs were "Help Yourself" and "Wasted." And "Todd's a Twit He Sucks His Dick," which was about Eric's deteriorating friendship with a guy named Todd, a local punk scenester whose sin was he did not rein in his personality to accommodate Eric's ego. Eric shouted, "Todd you really talk too much, that's why I hate your guts!" Glory to Eric for being honest. If anyone was going to talk too much, it was going to be Eric who had seen people laughing at Todd's jokes and appreciating Todd's punk style and humor—that was simply unacceptable!—but also Eric may have felt betrayed in that he saw Todd cozying up with other scenesters, hanging out with them, instead of him, and getting high and having fun. Eric sang, "You love your kiss-ass faggot friends, they'll buttfuck you in the end." To further denigrate Todd, the last line of his song went, "Why'd you turn so fucking gay?"

As for Todd, he was happy to have a whole song written about him.

Of course, Eric also wrote, "I Don't Care if You're Gay," which he may have presented as proof he wasn't homophobic, a term others used often to describe him. Why? Because he used the word "fag" a lot in just regular conversation, meaning it as an insult, sometimes, but also as a compliment or term of endearment, not so unlike, really, how the n-word was starting to gain traction as something you might get away with saying casually if you were Black. "You fag!" as in *How dare you be clever!* Or *funny* or *sneaky* or *cool.* You'd have to be pretty demented, or just out of things, to not know what he meant. The song was all so fast, all so astonishingly tight.

Another of Eric's songs, "Games," included the lyrics, "I can't deal with your games, all you faggots are lame," and, "Jealousy, is where it's at, you wanna be me, but you can't say that. I am the man with the master plan, and that's what makes me so goddamned grand."

The morning after the Hardcore Skate Party Eric sloshed the brand spanking new halfpipe with kerosene, burned it to the ground, got rid of the evidence. There'd been a serious accident the night before. Cops were sure to come snooping. The ramp was history.

20.

Hated Youth Plays Florida with D.R.I.

MARCH OF '84 WE TOURED the Sunshine State with Dirty Rotten Imbeciles from Texas whose 7" EP *Violent Pacification* about popped the top off the can of candied worms. It was that good. The album cover showed a skeleton in combat fatigues clutching an assault rifle with a bleeding baby skewered on the end of its bayonet—my kind of image! Also on the cover was the classic D.R.I. logo featuring a skanker put to line art, a transformation of the sloppy Circle Jerks skanker into an institutional framework. In the clean D.R.I. skanker stamp you saw something of a swastika. The music made the veins in our bodies writhe with joy.

Hated Youth's first act with D.R.I. was in Miami at good ole Flynn's Ocean 71, the sleazy nightclub doubling as hotel that we'd played before. Upon arriving, D.R.I. was in the lobby, there they were, standing there, and the guitarist, a guy named Spike, believe it or not, spoke of the poison that was heavy metal, how its sounds were penetrating the thrash scene. Spike made it seem as though nothing could be lower than mixing elements of metal in with your hardcore. Spike made it seem as though metal should be lodged at the bottom of a bog where it might lose hope and expire in a last exhale of impotent bubbles. A year or so later D.R.I. would take the stage in Tallahassee with their hair grown out and wearing Slayer t-shirts. Their next LP they would even title *Crossover*, their beloved skanker logo glistening as chrome. Was it possible? Yes, they would go on and do that, word getting around that they'd signed a three-million-dollar contract. Could it be?

Other bands had the same idea: S.S. Decontrol, Agnostic Front, even the incomparably fun-loving Suicidal Tendencies.

On a practical level, dropping metal into your thrash made sense. It gave you time to relax on stage. It panned out your set. Metal took less work, the result being you looked lazy, uncommitted, especially if you already were "strumming" your guitars instead of chafing them violently. If you had a Marshall half stack you could get away with mincing about on stage, plucking that pick up and down as though you had flipflops on, Bermuda shorts and a Panama hat—it still would pass as hardcore. And it might fool people into thinking it was fast. This observation I could not have made in 1984, but four decades later it was clear enough. There had been other hybrids developing too, poppy hardcore like with NOFX. Though the Bad Brains may have enjoyed reggae music, the extreme difference in pace gave the musicians, including the singer, time to rest as they geared up for their next song that pushed the limits of what was humanly possible. Also, the young guys in the bands may have been thinking about their futures. They were crossing over from their carefree youthful days into adulthood. Like what were they gonna do for the rest of their lives? If money was in metal, metal was the way to go, right?

Flynn's filled with people early, everybody in punk gear, many sitting at round tables set with candles burning inside red glass. These people spoke politely with each other, smoking cigarettes while others lounged in Naugahyde couches along the wall. The first band to play was Sector 4, who'd also come down from Tallahassee, and then Hated Youth played. When we finished our last song and were packing up, the guy who ran the place, Richard Shelter, said, "Wait, what do you guys think you're doing?" Eric said, "We're done." Shelter said, "No no, you can't stop playing now, you just started," so we amped back up and played through our set a second time.

During intermission, waiting for D.R.I. to go on, a blond woman in jeans pressed me to the wall with her breasts. I was taller than her. She had to look up at me, but her face was very close to mine. She said, "Do you have a girlfriend? I could be your girlfriend, you want me to be your girlfriend tonight, baby? I bet you already have a girl-friend, don't you? Damn, the good ones are always taken."

She talked along that way. I began to feel at ease. She seemed to want me to lift my hand and touch the place I had not touched since infancy. Call me the late bloomer. So I stroked one where it swelled whitely out of the top of her blouse, getting braver on the soft thing at each pass. But

D.R.I. broke into their set with "Violent Pacification." The urge to skank entered me like the Holy Spirit, as it did whenever I heard the metal crunch and crashing insanity. So I left her breast in the lurch, diving into the melee and hoping to look like the fleshed-out version of the D.R.I. logo.

D.R.I. followed "Violent Pacification" with "War Crimes" and then "Busted" and after that, "Draft Me." Like Hated Youth, most of their songs did not exceed a minute, and often didn't make it past 30 seconds. The four guys of the band looked as though they had just got off a construction site job, with loose jeans too long that bunched around the ankles, and worn-out Converse sneakers, the guitarist's faded blue, the bassist's faded red. The bassist wore a Felix the Cat shirt with the sleeves ripped off and his tuning keys were shaped after hearts. Behind the drums the drummer sported a black Cheap Trick shirt, stickers with skulls and symbols and the names of bands all over his kit: TOXIN III, Condemned to Death and Van Halen. All this while the singer, Kurt Brecht whose vocal timbre matched that of Nicholas Cage, jumped around shouting like a madman, his short hair done mange style where you take the buzzer and run it over your head randomly to achieve that rabid patchy look of amok insanity. I'd done it a few times myself.

Breathing fast from the hard skank I joined Eric and Tommy and David in front of the stage below the gushing clamor of D.R.I.'s imbecilic rage, the guitarist using picks stamped with the D.R.I. logo, his Les Paul hooked up to a Marshall half stack, the God of guitar amps. My disco-padded Kustom, by comparison, was but a lowly servant to the royal secretary.

Next day Eric and Brooke and I stepped onto the beach, flapped towels out over the sand and were taking in the rays. Near us, two Hispanic guys were chilling. They had a large bottle of sparkly liquid on hand, and drank from it while families strolled by, lilting children in bathing suits and folks who wanted to while the day away nicely in the ashtray. As the minutes passed on, the older guy stuck his face in the lap of the shirtless younger guy in jeans. They may have been trying to be discreet, but the booze had taken them into a sunshine fog of pubic hair and glistening bratwurst, or dream where they forgot about the world and were letting it all hang out. Three cops appeared, one a woman, to break up the blowjob. "Are you the *ee* or the *er*?" a cop asked several times angrily. The cops got the guys into cuffs while they were yet sitting, made them stand, then frogwalked them to their patrol cars.

The day before, an all-white jury had decided not to convict the Cuban-born cop who shot a Black guy in the face in '82, an incident that led to riots where a person died and dozens were hurt. Miami's Blacks, still pissed over the 1980 acquittal of 5 white cops who'd beaten one of their number to death with nightsticks and flashlights, were about sick of this shit. Who allowed these Hispanics to come in here and steal their jobs, anyway? Why did the *Cubanos* have the upper hand when it came to doling out justice? The acquittal added new salt to a long-festering injury—18 people had died in the 1980 riots—so the cops of Dade County were geared up to deal with a new round of assaults and unleashed hatred.

Our second night in Miami was weird as the first. Before the show even started, a cop saw Eric screech into the Flynn's parking lot in the punchy Chrysler Sebring he'd rented in Tallahassee. Eric started doing donuts and the cop called for backup. I was in the D.R.I. van with Tommy and David and the Dirty Rotten Imbeciles. We were passing a big fat joint while rolling new ones, the side doors open. Our thoughts were like, "There's Eric being Eric." It was amusing until four cop cars blasted into the lot, sirens wailing, and cut off all routes of escape. They had boxed us in. A cop jumped out with gun drawn. "Get out of the car, asshole!"

Eric got out while Brooke stayed in the passenger seat, alarmed and frustrated and fearful of what could happen.

The cop aimed the gun at Eric's French nose. The cop's arm was shaking.

"You have no reason to fear me," Eric said.

"Put your hands on the hood, do it now!" she screamed.

Eric, wearing a hoodie with a symbol on it evocative of a swastika, followed her instructions. On went the cuffs, Eric turning his head to the side in time to see Spike and Eric of D.R.I. dive into some bushes, doing major acrobatics to hide themselves. The cops frisked Eric. A dialogue began while the other cops pulled David and Tommy and I out of the van. Tommy had an ounce of weed in his pocket. Eric had an eightball of coke in the Sebring. The cops said the car matched the description of a car used that day in a bank robbery. Once they figured out the true nature of things—*oh, this guy is a musician, not a bank robber*—they got back in their cars and continued their searches for fresh eruptions of racial violence. Neither Tommy nor Eric were busted. A miracle.

Upon finishing our two sets, Tommy wanted to be alone, so went out on the beach behind the club. In the sand he came across a guy who said he'd just beat the shit out of his girlfriend in his car. The guy might've been drunk or on drugs, but Tommy wanted nothing to do with that kind of talk so came back to Flynn's Ocean 71 and sat in one of the couches in the hallway that ran between the club and lobby of the hotel. One of the girls he'd seen out on the beach, a punk girl in a short skirt, sat beside him and started snuggling on him, finally straddling him. We were like, "What's that girl doing to our bassist?" She pawed Tommy and squeezed his arm, all the while rubbing her cooch back and forth against his leg. The whole time she didn't say a word.

Our final morning, before setting off to Orlando for the next show, we went into a McDonalds. I ordered a hamburger. It was given to me. I unwrapped it in front of all of the people around and shouted, "Where's the beef?" like the old lady in the Wendy's commercial. I turned my head this way and that way, acting senile, like *Can you believe this? There's no meat in here.* "Where's the beef?" I kept saying, and the African-American girls laughed. *Oh, look at that white boy—he craze.*

Next we set up in Orlando at a place known as Rob and Regina's Warehouse. Again the cops came out. I had climbed a tree, see? In those days the sight of people with mohawks, let alone some guy with a mohawk hanging out in a tree, relaxing on a bough with one leg dangling down, was enough to draw cops into a tizzy. Cops hadn't gotten used to it. It was expected that they would arrive at some point. No, stupid, you're not allowed to take a nap in a tree! Get down from there, now!

Hated Youth at Rob and Regina's Warehouse, Orlando, 1984

Orlando's Dissent played first, then Bully Boys, a band into white superiority. They were part of a movement gaining momentum. If you look up the early Florida hardcore scene on YouTube you'll even find a clip of some young bald teenager who, knowing he is being videotaped, says, "Kill all n*****s" as though he means it—that may have been the attitude, give or take, of the Bully Boys. But when you saw Nazi skins hanging around, if they weren't kicking somebody in the shins or yanking an ex-girlfriend by the hair, they seemed more interested in brotherhood than hunting down and hurting Black people. In Tallahassee no real racist skinhead culture had appeared as of yet, not that we knew of, though we'd heard tell of it in places like California—the Dead Kennedys sang of it—and overseas skinhead bands like Skrewdriver were gaining followers.

Earlier, as we'd walked up the hill leading to the space, I'd seen the straight-backed chair set up outside the entrance. A skinhead in red suspenders and black boots stood there looking sharp and smiley, hair buzzer in hand. Before entering the building, folks sat in the chair—both skinhead regulars and wannabees—and got their skulls shaved down to the quick. The skins patted each other's shoulders as if they hadn't seen each other in months, and were damn happy to be together again, like they were part of a grand organization filled with a secret love you could only access after official acceptance. I had seen them in Jacksonville. Along with their combat boots they liked to sport flight jackets with confederate flags sewn into the arms. I had seen them at the Minor Threat and Necros shows in Gainesville. On the surface they appeared rough and tumble, like a clean-shaven club of merry jokesters. In reality they were much darker.

The Bully Boys played well. Somebody there described them as a garage band. Though they may have expressed violent intentions directed at Blacks and Jewish people and people who did not possess their own physical qualities, the lyrics were buried in commotion and sound. A few years later, some kids of a like mind would set a homeless man on fire in Saint Pete and burn him to death. Had I known how invested the Bully Boys were in "white stuff," how it wasn't pretend or for show, I may have felt embarrassed standing there watching. Had I been born under a different star, I might even have been angry.

Our brother band from Tallahassee, the thrashy, sometimes psychedelic-sounding, Reagan-fuckyouing always fun to watch Sector 4 played next. Then Hated Youth took the stage to a fierce pit. Skinheads hopped up with us and dived into the crowd. When D.R.I. began, somebody set up an exercise trampoline that the skinheads used to launch themselves onto the stage from which they then jumped back into the crowd.

I would come across the leader of the Bully Boys a year or so later when T.S.O.L. played with the Drills and Belching Penguin at the Cuban Club in Ybor City. I had been taking photographs, getting some good ones of him strongarming some punk with a tall mohawk. Later that night, sitting at the CC bar with him, he asked if I liked MDC. I said, "Sure, yeah, they're great," realizing weeks later that that was not the answer he was hoping for. From the skinhead POV, anyone who could like Millions of Dead Cops, or Multi Death Corporation, or whatever they were calling themselves at that time in their criticisms of the American Way, was either soft or some crank worth bludgeoning, not to mention "gay," which was the case for MDC's singer. I think the Bully Boy, knowing I had been one of the guys from Hated Youth, saw that I was ignorant of the skinhead lifestyle and cause, felt sorry for me, and so spared me the harassment that may have followed such a declaration.

While playing Rob and Regina's Warehouse, Tommy, our resident sasquatch with the long hippy hair, had to use the headstock of his Rickenbacker to push people off him. After busting a few heads he realized he may have hurt somebody, may have committed violence, what a horrible thing to have done! *Oh ye gentle sasquatches of the world.* Shit gave Tommy a guilt trip. Tommy felt bad about it. But people got hurt here and there along the way, didn't they? People got their eyes ripped out, their eyeballs stomped on, their sight splashed with boiling radiator fluid. Broken noses, broken necks, bruised limbs, cracked bones, a confusion over what happens next. It all was part of the punk rock enterprise.

21.

The Murder of a Girl

SENIOR YEAR AT SOAR I bought a 400cc Kawasaki street bike with money made working for the throat surgeon who said God wanted men to hunt and gather and work the land, not just develop and use their intellects. The godly life took faith *and* physical exertion, and that is why he spent so much time caring for cows, planting pine trees, and renovating old trailers to rent to poor white people, all while meeting with patients, performing surgeries, and staying active in the church. As a believer, the doctor was compelled to share his wisdom, speaking occasionally of his agreement with Noah's curse against Ham's son while passing on lessons in frugality, parsimony, strength-building and the common sense he saw missing from the modern world. Did parents teach kids to wash from the top down? Did parents say no to buying pencils in that pencils could be picked off sidewalks for free each and every day of the week?

No? Well, why the hell not?

The doctor shared do-it-yourself principles in industry, impressing on me the value of saving discarded objects that might be repurposed in future days. Cinder blocks could be used for dumbbells. A plastic soda pop bottle could be sawn in two, one half used for a funnel, the other half used as a bowl. This mentality would save me the hours and expenses attached to buying stuff you didn't really need, or only needed marginally. You'd have to be a fool to buy a lighter in that lighters were all over the place. Just pick one up and give it a roll of the thumb. Chances were a flame would pop right on out. The same was true for things like hairbands, kitchenware and toenail clippers. If you needed any of that stuff, wait until you found it already. The doc was well-to-do yet if he stumbled across a dime, he would lean over. You'd see him pick it up and put it in his pocket.

The only advice my dad gave me, and he gave it only once, was never read the same book twice. Though my dad may have imparted a few useful lessons through example, he had better things to do than fuck around with kids, of which he had way too many, a whopping five sons. How much better to delve deeper into Diogenes of Sinope, how exciting, and Socrates, Nietzsche, Machiavelli and Jesus. In retrospect, it would have been nice to have been inculcated in Marxism, heavy-duty revolutionary anti-imperialism, Magónism, Stalinism, Communism and the other isms our father loved with such passion.

Had I been politically-minded, would I have bypassed the slight feelings of cringe I got when bands—even the Dead Kennedys sometimes—took up positions against the government, or presented, *à la* Bad Religion and Reagan

Youth, roundup calls for social change? It was natural to complain of your government, wasn't it? Of Reagan and the Freedom Fighters in El Salvador? Why, then, did songs against the government and other easy targets—racism, war, destruction of the environment—make me feel a tiny bit embarrassed, especially since punk rock and left-wing politics went so well together? There was the assumption: if you're listening, you believe this too, you're one of us. But I was a guy who, if I saw somebody doing something I was doing, felt inclined to stop doing that thing. I couldn't stand the sense of mandatory unity, the nausea whose influence I fought by pretending I was unlike other people. Despite the "fight for good" and catchy funtime, sometimes frolicsomeness of a lot of those political punk songs—MDC's "Born to Die" as a prime example, or the wonderful MDC song professing a dying love for Nancy Reagan—this thread of punk rock felt arbitrarily dogmatic, like another form of conformity, take your pick, yellow or green.

And why did no songs (though there may have been some) mention Israel's part in splattering Muslim blood across walls in Beirut in 1982, of using napalm and phosphorous bombs?

That's not a question.

Nor is it a statement.

A real cynic might say there's no way out, that hypocrisy and bloodlust and trickery are permanent features of us. Just if you're going to be *that kind* of political, why not go *all the way?*

The doctor let me whack his weeds, fix his fences, insulate his pipes. He paid me to feed his peacocks, cows, swans, alligators. I mowed his grass, picked figs from his tree. I shoveled rocks out of his truck bed, dug ditches, planted sapling pines, burned fields and sowed seed. Had all this been taking place in the old days, around 1850 during Florida's 20 years of being a Slave State, I would have been the surgeon's overseer. I would have been his slave driver.

The doctor worked me hard. Each task I hit with gusto. He was proud, and told my mom, "Because he can work for me, he'll be able to work for anybody for the rest of his life." Of the mohawks Eric and I sported while flying along in the back of his pickup truck those days we worked for him together, the doctor found it unusual but respected it. On occasion he would happen upon a farmer friend while driving up McCracken Road, a dirt road east of town that led to one of his properties. He would stop in the road and the two farmers would talk to each other, truck window to truck window. To explain away the strange-looking guys in the back of his truck, he would say, "Yeah, those hair styles are a gimmick for their band," and he would say, "Tomahawk," summing Hated Youth up in a word. In this likening of us to the noble pursuits of the Indians of yore, he ran his flattened hand through the air like a tomahawk. It was the same gesture Florida State University football team fans used en masse at the games, everybody waving arms in the stands as though pledging allegiance to the Führer, only lower key, a simple chest level *thwack*, the kind used to sever a person's scalp.

Eric did not last long working for the doctor, two months tops, for the doctor had put Eric on the riding mower in front of his great house where the cast iron yard jockey greeted visitors by lantern. Eric's job was simple enough just he neglected to lift the mower deck while rolling over a stump. Eric messed up the blade so the doctor had to school Eric. Eric did not like being schooled.

This doctor, my accidental mentor, cherished his ancestral history and was of the mind we'd be better off had the South won the war. This was my role model. Good thing, then, that I remained wishy-washy. Good thing, then, that Eric, through his authoritative narcissistic confidence presented another quasi-father-figure, one to help anchor me with a purposeful direction. Without my friend Eric who knows where this haplessly floating stoner boy that was I would have drifted?

Being in the band set my course. With Eric I had a community with an object other than merely getting high, a design that would guide me into a life of starving artistry, as people said, not a good thing exactly but it was better than nothing. Years later, after we had been apart for a while but then were friends for a second time around in Tallahassee, Eric would say, "You are the cre-ay-*tor*, I am the appreci-ay-*tor*.

I was the creator, he was the appreciator.

Maybe, just maybe, I liked being appreciated.

On my Kawasaki motorcycle I zipped in and out of the SOAR parking lot, too cool for school, wearing the leather jacket I bought, also, with money earned working for the racist doctor. Here was—yes, I'll say it—an identity in the making, and I clung to it. I was a loner with a group. I no longer had to feel alienated from the social workings of the world I was born into and required to participate in. I could do like Nancy Reagan had said in reference to recreational drug use (JUST SAY NO), dismissing not crack cocaine but the sources of my experiences in rejection: school, classmates, parents, neighbors. Just say no to Lynyrd Skynyrd. Just say no to high school graduation ceremonies. Goodbye jocks, goodbye school, to the devil with people who smoked cigarettes, and the churches and government institutions. For good measure I lumped everything I could sneer at into the same group, imagining there was, as in Willy Wonka's chocolate factory, an ejection button I could press to get rid of the "bad eggs." Call it preventative rejection, or movement from the position of the rejected to one with power to reject. Before the band, before exercising our creativity, nobody on the planet would have seen me as valuable in any way. Or so it felt.

In my emboldened state I was naïve enough and dumb enough to ignore the voice inside saying something was off. Under my look and sometimes antisocial behavior was a knowledge that meaning could only ever be illusory. Under the look the isolated introvert who wanted to join life's club remained.

Hated Youth would play another out-of-town show—with Negative Approach, Iron Cross and Beyond Therapy in Gainesville—but our final show in Tallahassee was at the Downunder on the campus of FSU just off the quad where we had, as the Little Johnnys, first shared our creativity publicly. Of the Downunder show somebody named Robert Chitwood wrote a letter to the college paper. The paper published Chitwood's letter on April 20, 1984. Of Hated Youth's last Tallahassee show Chitwood said:

Congrats to Hated Youth and the slammers at the Downunder this last Friday night for creating the first successful (if short), slam event I've seen in Tallahassee. Slamming is Fun. Slamming is about movement, fun and mutual support – not being jerks and elbowing people in the face. Thanks for keeping it the former, not the latter. As one participant put it, "It's more fun than roller derby!" Special thanks to Hated Eric for being responsible and helping clear the dance floor when a beer bottle was dropped. One thing, Eric. Stop making comments about "faggots." If a hardcore stance requires mandatory outrage, take it to Reagan, nukes, your boss, Billy Idol, or Mommy, someplace there may be a real threat or grudge, not "fags" and Jonny Rotten. People like these cleared the space you can act outrageous in. If you want to suffer from trendy homophobia, keep it to yourself.

Hated Youth at the Downunder, 1984

Three days later and roughly a month before I graduated from the School of Analytical Reasoning, a girl was beaten over the head with a flute in a field near a lake in the town. The event was like something from one of our songs, for hadn't we sung about Theodore Bundy who'd come into our town to rip a post off the headboard of a sorority girl's bed? From what I understood, Bundy shoved the post up between her legs. Then he yanked it out of her body and slammed it over the head of another girl sleeping nearby, an act that had to have been spontaneous, improvised. It was the DIY approach to murdering women.

The guy who killed the girl, the paper said, tried having sex with her but she refused and that's when he beat her to death with her flute and left her in the field, her body visible from the road, like if you were driving along you could look over there and see a lump of girl in the field. It wasn't all that far from the drainage ditch where on occasion I skated joyfully with my skater pals. The flute murderer was the girl's classmate, a fellow student at Lincoln High, someone I would have assumed was a jock, but no, nope, and negative. The killer, the paper said, was a loner, like me.

For me, the Melissa Bean murder had the quality of a conclusion and harbinger. The band was over, high school was ending, but something was beginning. In this moment I could have looked at everything in my life that had happened so far and made decisions on how to proceed wisely, but no, nope and negative. The end of the summer came around. Still seventeen, I hopped on my bike. Wearing the leather jacket from Sears, I rode to Daytona Beach, my mother driving behind me in her car loaded with musical gear, my clothes, and the new cameras I was to use during my stretch as a student at the Southeast Center for Photographic Studies. My mom and I that evening walked along the beach together. In the morning we visited a realtor who hooked me up in a one-room garage apartment five blocks from the ocean. This was a place, the realtor said, where teenaged prostitution was rampant. No problem there. I held out my hand and he gave me the keys.

22.
TALLAHASSEE ALBUM
1984 – 1988

Note: *These photos were taken inside and around Ca Chapel at 812 S. Macomb St., but also at the Musical Moon and a few house parties and an Island Water Sports event behind Gumby's Pizza.*

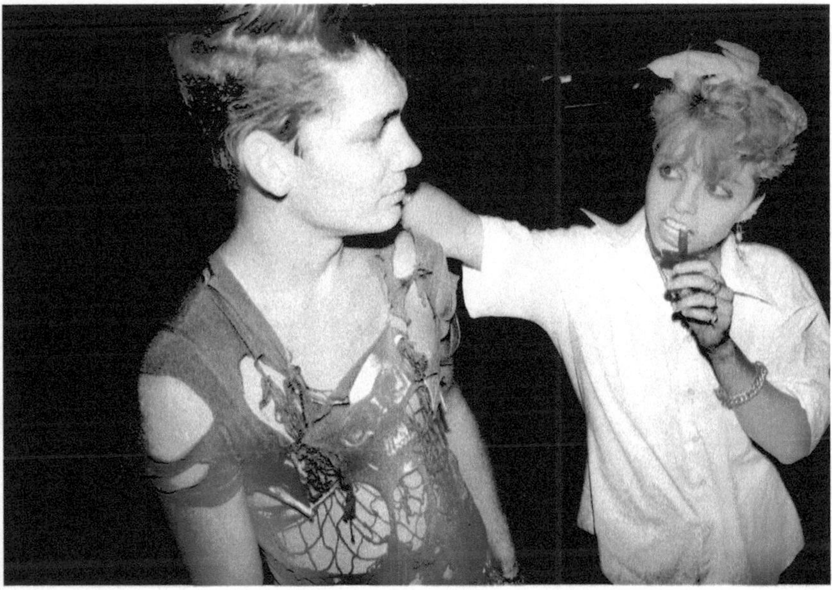

WELCOME TO
CHAPEL

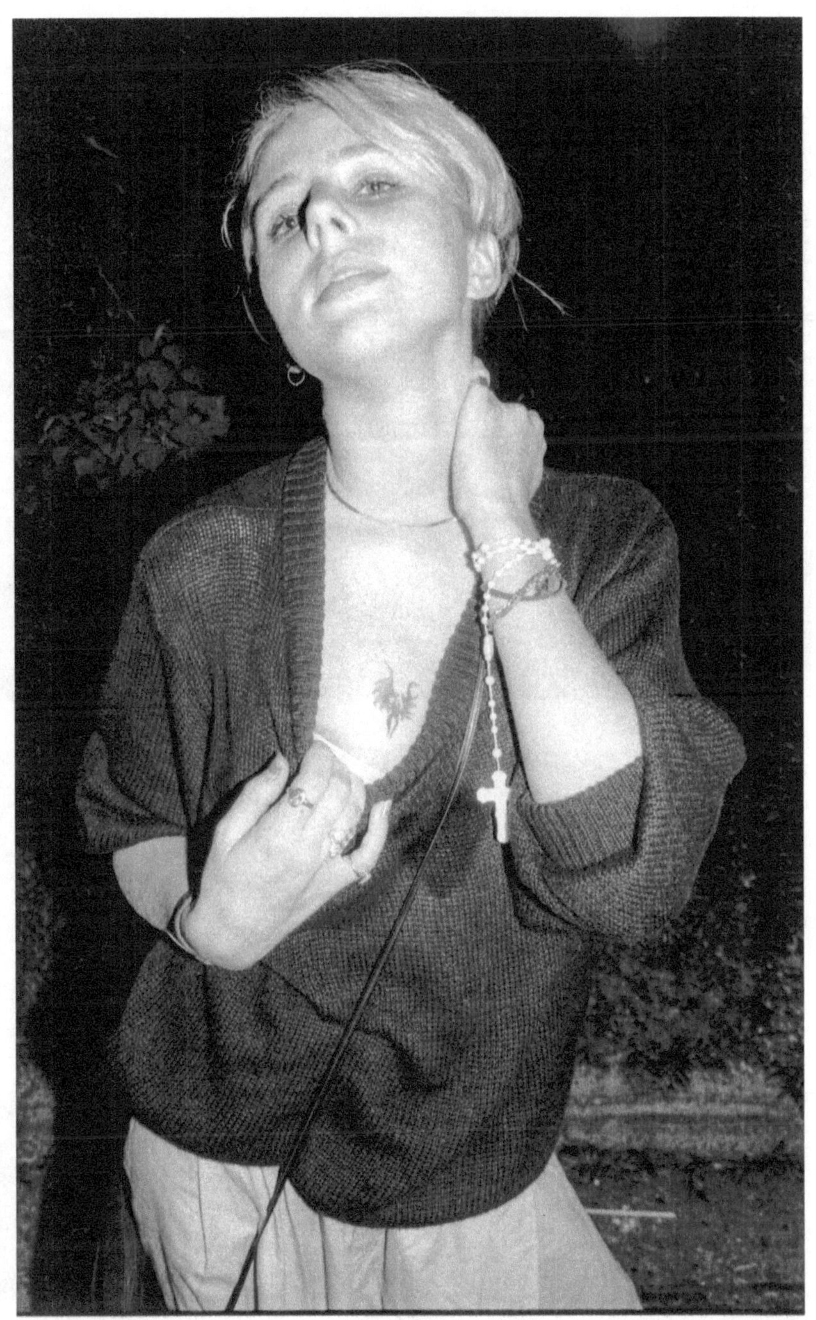

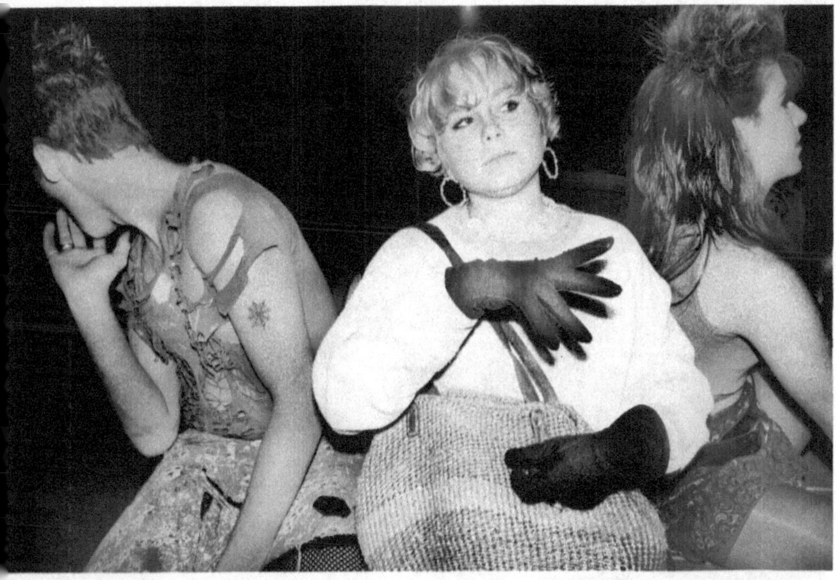

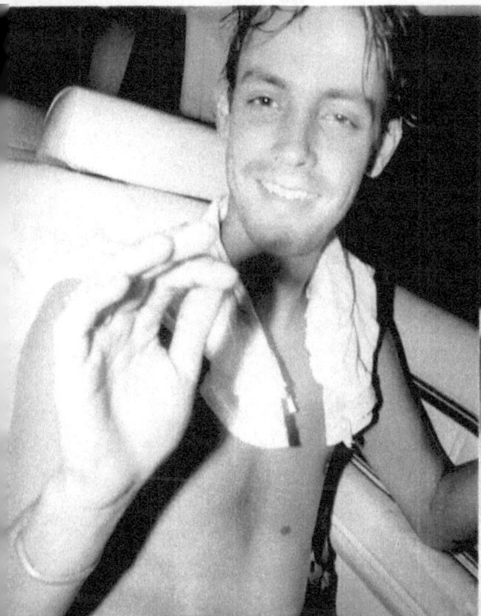

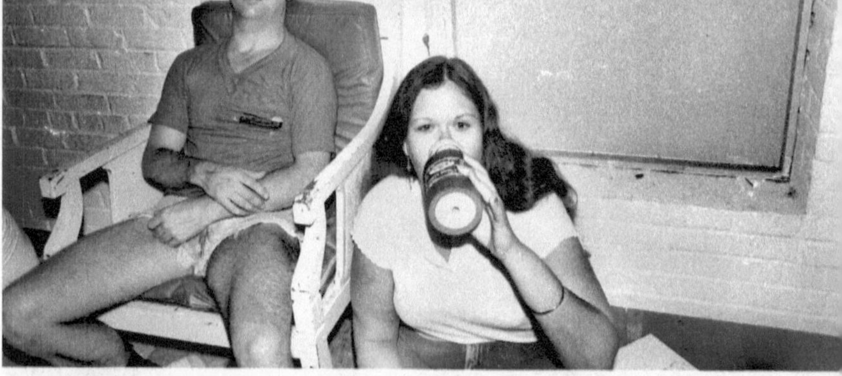

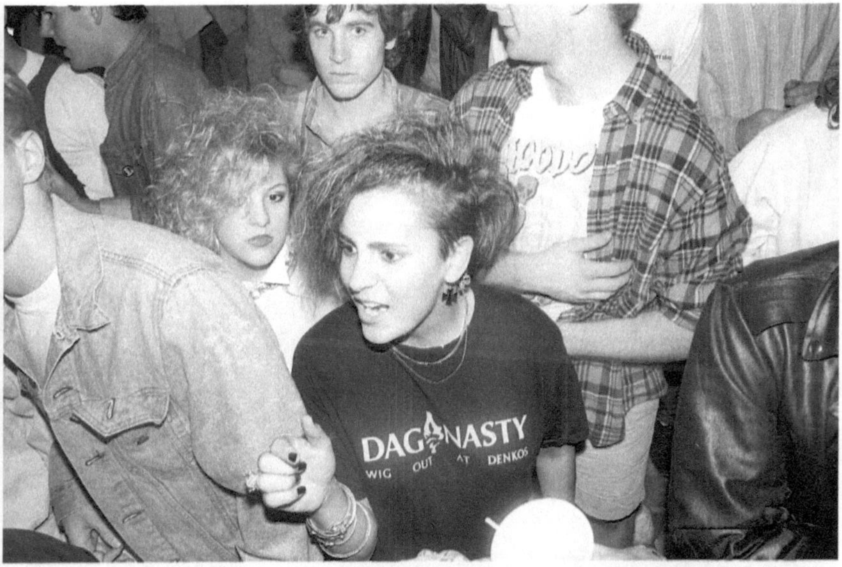
DAG NASTY
WIG OUT AT DENKOS

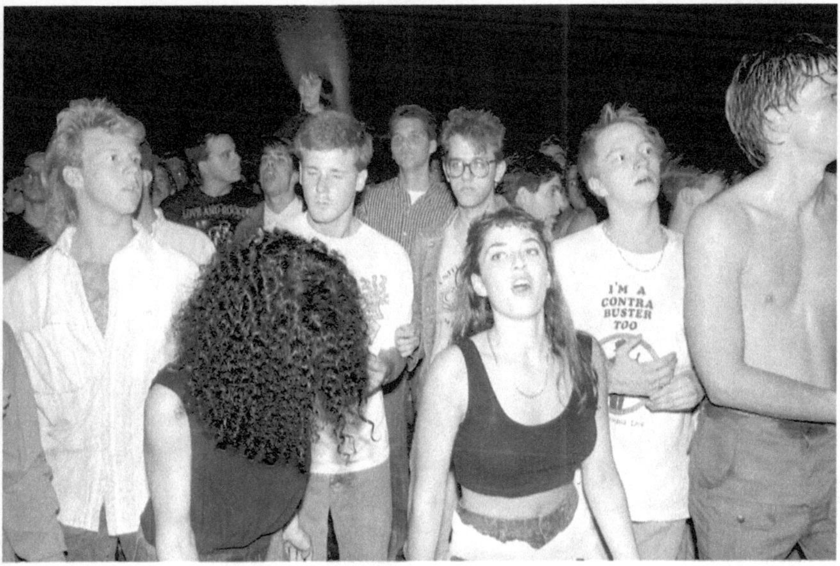
I'M A
CONTRA
BUSTER
TOO

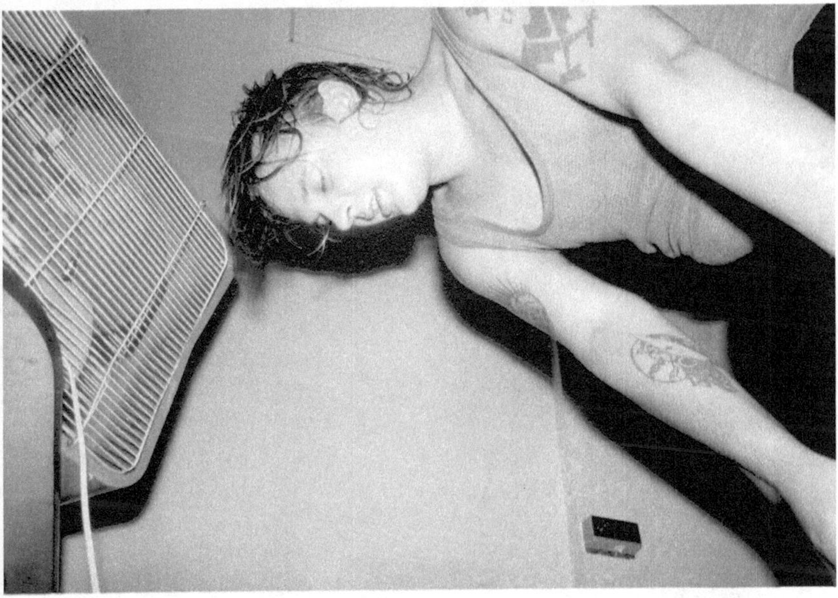

EXIT

NO
GOD
CARLO

ADAM STRAUS
FOR U.S. SENATE
ADAM STRAUS
FOR U.S. SENATE
T-SHIRTS
M-L-XL
ALBUMS
$5,—
lute to
edom

KILL THE PUNKS

END

Acknowledgements

Musicians and showgoers from Tallahassee's underground music scene during the 1980s contributed to this project. Hated Youth's Gary Strickland helped with research and shared detailed recollections, as did Hated Eric (RIP). Others who helped are: Lucia Cartledge (RIP), David McKee (RIP), Jon Cox (RIP), Kris Dorris (RIP), Karen Hawthorne (RIP), Tommy Hamilton, Alain Rodgers, Paul and Neal and Greg from Sector 4, Amy Pike, Margaret Van Every, Danny Heinze. Thank you Shane and Dylan Quigley, Todd Gulledge, Jeff Walsh Farnum, Lou Perdomo, George Barker, Bonny Lorie Dotson, and Mallory Bevis, DeAnn Caughey, Bruce Fain, Phil Coppage (RIP), Ken Collins, Donny Crenshaw, and Nancy O'Bryant. Apologies to Ray McKelvey (RIP), singer for Stevie Stiletto and the Switchblades. Thank you Bob Suren of Burrito Records for releasing Hated Youth on vinyl in the two-thousands, and for writing about Hated Youth in *Crate Digger: An Obsession with Punk Records*. Appreciation to Jeff Hodapp of Destroy Records for permission to quote Roach Motel lyrics. Benisons to reporters at large: Steve Dollar, Jay Murphy, Henri Cawthon, Christopher Farrell, Robert Chitwood; and bless Ms. Moon whose blog (*Bless Our Hearts*) contains early memories of Smitty's Club. Thank you Damien Filer and Jon Bleyer of Panhandle Punk Productions for their inspiring interest in Tallahassee music history. Mike and Zilpha Underwood were crucial personalities in the support of and development of Hated Youth and Daughter Damage. And thank you SAIL (School for Applied Individualized Learning) for giving me the "paybacks" I deserved. Photos on pages 161, 173, and 183 are by Sue Galvin. All other photos are by the author. Front cover is of Hated Eric in Atlanta, GA, early morning following a Hated Youth performance. Back cover shows Hated Eric, that same morning, skateboarding down Luckie Street.

WASP LEG PRESS
Books That Sting